The Woman Was [...] As Gorgeous, Dave Realized.

And not above pulling rank over him. Well, that pretty much fit in with what he'd heard about Lieutenant Commander Kate Hargrave.

The sexy hurricane hunter couldn't know it but her ex-husband had had a few things to say to Dave about the woman who'd just dumped him, none of them particularly flattering. She was, according to the still-bitter aviator, ambitious as hell, fearless in the air, a tiger in bed and a real ball-buster out of it.

Dave figured three out of four was good enough for him.

Yes, sir, he thought, as he caught a last glimpse of turquoise spandex in the mirror. This assignment was looking better and better by the minute.

Dear Reader,

Welcome to another compelling month of powerful, passionate and provocative love stories from Silhouette Desire. You asked for it…you got it…more Dynasties! Our newest continuity, DYNASTIES: THE DANFORTHS, launches this month with Barbara McCauley's *The Cinderella Scandal.* Set in Savannah, Georgia, and filled with plenty of family drama and sensuality, this new twelve-book series will thrill you for the entire year.

There is one sexy air force pilot to be found between the pages of the incomparable Merline Lovelace's *Full Throttle,* part of her TO PROTECT AND DEFEND series. And the fabulous Justine Davis is back in Silhouette Desire with *Midnight Seduction,* a fiery tale in her REDSTONE, INCORPORATED series.

If it's a whirlwind Vegas wedding you're looking for (and who isn't?) then be sure to pick up the third title in Katherine Garbera's KING OF HEARTS miniseries, *Let It Ride.* The fabulous TEXAS CATTLEMAN'S CLUB: THE STOLEN BABY series continues this month with Kathie DeNosky's tale of unforgettable passion, *Remembering One Wild Night.* And finally, welcome new author Amy Jo Cousins to the Desire lineup with her superhot contribution, *At Your Service.*

I hope all of the Silhouette Desire titles this month will fulfill your every fantasy.

Melissa Jeglinski

Melissa Jeglinski
Senior Editor, Silhouette Desire

Please address questions and book requests to:
Silhouette Reader Service
U.S.: 3010 Walden Ave., P.O. Box 1325, Buffalo, NY 14269
Canadian: P.O. Box 609, Fort Erie, Ont. L2A 5X3

MERLINE LOVELACE

FULL THROTTLE

Silhouette® Desire

Published by Silhouette Books

America's Publisher of Contemporary Romance

SILHOUETTE BOOKS

ISBN 0-373-76556-8

FULL THROTTLE

Copyright © 2004 by Merline Lovelace

Visit Silhouette at www.eHarlequin.com

Printed in U.S.A.

Books by Merline Lovelace

MERLINE LOVELACE

spent twenty-three years in the air force, pulling tours in Vietnam, at the Pentagon and at bases all over the world. When she hung up her uniform, she decided to try her hand at writing. She's since had more than fifty novels published, with over seven million copies of her work in print. She and her husband enjoy traveling and chasing little white balls around the fairways. Watch for the next book in the *TO PROTECT AND DEFEND* series, *The Right Stuff*, coming from Silhouette Intimate Moments in March 2004.

To my buds on the RomVets loop—
women who all served their country and are now
turning out great novels! Thanks for sharing your
expertise on aircraft malfunctions, explosive devices
and general all around fun stuff.

One

Kate Hargrave was a good five miles into her morning jog when she spotted a plume of dust rising from the desert floor. Swiping at the sweat she'd worked up despite the nip September had brought to the high desert, she squinted through the shimmering New Mexico dawn at the vehicle churning up that long brown rooster tail.

A senior weather researcher with the National Oceanographic and Atmospheric Agency, Kate had logged hundreds of hours of flight time as one of NOAA's famed Hurricane Hunters. The pilots she flew with all possessed a steady hand on the controls, nerves of steel and an unshakable belief in their ability to look death in the eye and stare it down. So when she gauged the speed of the pickup hurtling straight toward her, she had no doubt who was at its wheel.

USAF Captain Dave Scott—a seasoned test pilot with hundreds of hours in both rotary and fixed-wing aircraft. Scott had been yanked off an assignment with Special Operations to become the newest addition to the supersecret test cadre tucked away in this remote corner of southeastern New Mexico.

He was supposed to have arrived last night but had phoned Captain Westfall from somewhere along the road and indicated he'd check in first thing this morning. No explanations for the delay, or none the navy captain in charge of the supersecret Pegasus project had relayed to his crew, anyway.

That alone was enough to put a dent in Kate's characteristically sunny good nature. She and the rest of the small, handpicked cadre had been here for weeks now. They'd been working almost around the clock to conduct final operational testing on the new all-weather, all-terrain attack-assault vehicle code-named Pegasus. The urgency of their mission had been burned into their brains from day one. That Captain Scott would delay his arrival—even by as little as eight hours of admittedly dead time—didn't particularly sit well with Kate.

Then there was the fact that the air force had pegged Scott to replace Lieutenant Colonel Bill

Thompson, the original air force representative to the project. Everyone on the team had liked and respected the easygoing and highly experienced test pilot. Unfortunately, Bill had suffered a heart attack after being infected by the vicious virus that attacked him and a number of other members of the test cadre some days ago.

Now Bill was off the Pegasus project and probably off flying status for the rest of his life. His abrupt departure had ripped a gaping hole in the tight, close team of officers and civilians plucked from all branches of the military to work on the project. Dave Scott would have to scramble to catch up with the rest of the test cadre *and* prove himself worthy to fill Bill Thompson's boots.

"Sure hope you're up to it, fella."

With that fervent wish, Kate lengthened her stride. She'd just as soon not come face-to-face with her new associate out here in the desert. Her hair was a tangled mess and her turquoise spandex running suit sported damp patches of sweat. With luck and a little more oomph to her pace, she could veer off onto the dirt track that ringed the perimeter of the site before Scott hit the first checkpoint.

She should have known she couldn't outrun a sky jock. The speeding pickup skidded to a stop at the checkpoint while Kate was still some distance from the perimeter trail.

The dazzling light shooting through the peaks of

the Guadalupe Mountains off to the east illuminated the vehicle. The truck was battered. Dust streaked. An indeterminate color between blue and gray. She couldn't see the driver, though. He was still too far away and the bright rays glinting off the windshield formed an impenetrable shield.

She'd get a glimpse of him soon enough, Kate guessed wryly. From the bits and pieces of background information she'd gathered about Captain Dave Scott, she knew he wasn't the type to cruise by a female in a tight jogging suit. Or one in support hose and black oxfords, for that matter. Rumor had it Scott was the love-'em-and-leave-'em type, with a string of satisfied lovers stretching from coast to coast.

Kate knew the breed.

All too well.

So she wasn't surprised when the pickup cleared the checkpoint, roared into gear and kicked up dust for another quarter mile or so. Scant yards from Kate, it fishtailed to a halt once more.

Dust swirled. The truck's engine idled with a low, throaty growl. The driver's-side window whirred down. A well-muscled forearm appeared, followed by a rugged profile. With his creased straw cowboy hat and sun-weathered features, Scott might have been one of the locals who'd adapted so well to life here in the high desert. The hat shaded the upper portion of his face. The lower portion consisted of the tip of a nose, a mouth bracketed by laugh lines and a blunt, square chin. The rolled sleeve of his white cotton shirt showed a sprinkling of hair bleached to gold by the sun. Mirrored aviator sunglasses shielded his eyes, but the grin he flashed Kate was pure sex.

"Well, well." The drawl was deep and rich and carried clearly on the morning air. "This assignment is looking better by the moment."

Kate had heard variations of the same line a hundred or more times in her career. Her ready smile, flaming auburn hair and generous curves had attracted the attention of every male she'd ever worked with. She'd long ago learned to separate the merely goggling from the seriously annoying and handle both with breezy competence. Edging to the side of the dirt road, she jogged toward the idling vehicle. Her voice held only dry amusement as she offered a word of advice.

"Pull in your tongue and hit the gas pedal, flyboy. Captain Westfall's expecting you."

His chin dipped. Eyes a clear, startling blue peered over the rim of the sunglasses and locked with hers.

"The captain can wait," he replied. "You, on the other hand…"

He didn't finish. Or if he did, Kate didn't hear him.

She'd kept her gaze engaged with his a half second too long and run right off the edge of the road.

Her well-worn Nikes came down not on hard-packed dirt, but empty air. With a smothered oath, she plunged into the shallow ditch beside the road. Her right leg hit with a jar that rattled every bone in her body before going out from under her. A moment later she landed smack on her rear atop a fat, prickly tumbleweed.

So much for breezy competence!

Scott was out of the pickup almost before Kate and the tumbleweed connected. His low-heeled boots scattered rock and dirt as he scrambled into the shallow depression. When he hunkered down beside her, she expected at least a minimal expression of concern. What she got was a swift, assessing glance followed by a waggle of his sun-streaked eyebrows.

"And here I woke up this morning thinking the next few weeks were going to be all work and no play."

Kate cocked an eyebrow. Best to set him straight right here, right now. "You thought right, Captain."

"I don't know about that." Dipping his chin, he gave her another once-over. "Things are lookin' good from where I'm squatting. *Very* good."

Kate sucked in a swift breath. Behind their screen of sun-bleached lashes, his eyes were electric blue. The little white lines at their corners disappeared when he smiled, which he did with devastating effect.

Thank heavens she'd been inoculated against Scott's brand of lazy charm and cocky self-assurance.

The inoculation had been painful, sure, but once administered was supposed to last a lifetime.

Unfortunately, she hadn't been inoculated against the effects of sharp, stinging barbs to the backside. The prickly weed had penetrated right through her spandex running tights. Now that Kate had recovered from the initial shock of her fall, she felt its sharp, stinging bite.

"How about unsquatting," she suggested dryly, "and helping me up?"

"My pleasure."

Rising with the careless grace of an athlete, he reached for her hand. His palm felt tough and callused against her skin, his skin warm to the touch.

Of course Kate's blasted ankle had to give out the moment she gained her feet. With a grunt, she fell right into his conveniently waiting arms. This time he had the decency to show some concern. At least that was the excuse he gave for swooping her up.

"You must have come down hard on that ankle."

Hefting her not-inconsiderable weight, he cradled her against his chest. His very solid, very muscled chest, Kate couldn't help noticing.

"I'd better get you to the base."

He was already out of the ditch and striding around the back of the pickup before she could tell him she had a more pressing problem to worry about than her ankle. She tried to think of a subtle way to inform him of her dilemma. None came immediately to mind. Sighing, she stopped him just as he opened the passenger door and prepared to deposit her inside.

"Before you plop me down on that seat, I think you should know I'm sporting a collection of needle-sharp stickers. I landed on a tumbleweed," she added when he flashed her a startled look. "I need to remove a few unwanted thistles from my posterior."

"Damn!" His mouth took a wicked curve. "And I was just thinking my day couldn't get any better."

His leer was so exaggerated, she didn't even try to hold back her sputter of laughter. "Let's not make this any more embarrassing than it already is. Just put me down and I'll, er, perform an emergency extraction."

He set her on her feet and gave her a hopeful look. "I'll be glad to assist in the operation."

"I can manage."

Making no effort to hide his disappointment, he watched with unabashed interest while Kate grabbed the door handle to steady herself and twisted around. It took some contorting to reach all the thorny stickers. One by one, she flicked them off into the ditch.

"You missed one," Scott advised as she dusted the back of her thigh. "A little lower."

Removing the last twig, she leaned her weight on her ankle to test it. The pain was already subsiding, thank goodness. Pasting a smile on her face, she turned to her would-be rescuer.

"I'm Lieutenant Commander Kate Hargrave, by

the way. I'm with the National Oceanographic and Atmospheric Agency.''

As a lieutenant commander in NOAA's commissioned-officer corps, Kate outranked an air force captain. The fact that Scott had just watched a senior officer pluck thorns out of her bottom appeared to afford him no end of amusement. His eyes glinting between those ridiculously thick gold-tipped lashes, he introduced himself.

''Dave Scott. Airplane driver.''

To her profound disgust, Kate discovered her inoculation against handsome devils like this one wasn't quite as effective as she'd thought. Or as permanent. Shivers danced along her skin as she gazed up at him. He was so close she could see the beginnings of a bristly gold beard. The way his cheeks creased when he smiled. The reflection of her sweat-sheened face in his mirrored glasses.

She got an up close whiff of him, too. Unlike Kate, he still carried a morning-shower scent, clean and shampooy, coated with only a faint tang of dust. No woodsy aftershave for Captain Dave Scott, she noted, then wondered why the heck she'd bothered to take such a detailed inventory.

This wasn't smart, Kate thought as her heart thumped painfully against her ribs. Not smart at all. She'd learned the hard way not to trust too-handsome charmers like this one. If nothing else, her brief, disastrous marriage had taught her to go with her head and not her hormones where men were concerned.

Added to that was the fact that she and Scott would be working together for the next few weeks. In extremely close proximity. Despite her flamboyant looks and sensual figure, Kate was a professional to her toes. A woman didn't acquire a long string of initials after her name and the title of senior weather research scientist at the National Oceanographic and Atmospheric Agency without playing the game by the rules.

"Do Not Fool Around With the Hired Help" ranked right up there as rule number two. Or maybe it was three. Within the top five, anyway.

Not that Kate was thinking about fooling around with Captain Dave Scott. Just the opposite! Still, goose bumps danced along her spine as he took her elbow to assist her into the pickup's passenger seat. Once she was comfortably ensconced, he rounded the front end of the truck and climbed behind the wheel.

"So how long have you been on-site?" he asked, putting the vehicle into gear.

"From day one."

When his boot hit the gas pedal, Kate braced herself for the thrust. Instead of jerking forward, however, the pickup seemed to coil its legs like some powerful, predatory beast and launched into a silent run. Obviously, Scott had installed one heck of an engine inside the truck's less-than-impressive frame.

Interesting, she thought. The captain was a whole lot like his vehicle. All coiled muscle and heart-stopping blue eyes under a battered straw cowboy hat and rumpled white shirt.

"So what's the skinny?" he asked. "Is Pegasus ready to fly?"

Instantly, Kate's thoughts shifted from the man beside her to the machine housed in a special hangar constructed of materials designed to resist penetration by even the most sophisticated spy satellites.

"Almost," she replied. "Bill Thompson had his heart attack just as we were finishing ground tests."

"I never met Thompson, but I've heard of him. The AF lost a damned good pilot."

"Yes, it did. So did Pegasus. You've got a lot of catching up to do," she warned him, "and not much time to do it."

"No problem."

The careless reply set Kate's jaw. She and the rest of the cadre had been hard at it for weeks now. If Scott thought he was going to waltz in and get up to speed on the top secret project in a few hours, he had one heck of a surprise waiting for him.

Unaware that he'd just scratched her exactly the wrong way, the captain seemed more interested in Kate than the project that would soon consume him.

"I saw your career brief in the package headquarters sent as part of my orientation package. Over a thousand hours in the P-3. That's pretty impressive."

It was, by Kate's standards as well as Scott's. Only the best of the best got to fly aboard NOAA's specially configured fleet of aircraft, including the P–3 Orion. Flying into the eye of a howling hurricane took guts, determination and a cast-iron stomach. Honesty forced Kate to add a qualifier, though.

"Not all those hours were hurricane time. Occasionally we saw blue sky."

"I went up once with the air force's Hurricane Hunters based at Keesler."

Kate stiffened. Her ex-husband was assigned to the Air Force Reserve unit at Keesler Air Force Base, on Mississippi's Gulf Coast. That's where she'd met John, during a conference that included all agencies involved in tracking and predicting the fury unleashed all too often on the Gulf by Ma Nature.

That's also where she'd found the jerk with his tongue down the mouth of a nineteen-year-old bimbette. Kate had few fond memories of Keesler.

"So how was your flight?" she asked, shoving aside the reminder of her most serious lapse in judgment.

"Let's just say once was enough."

"Flying into a maelstrom of wind and rain isn't for the faint of heart," she agreed solemnly.

He cracked a grin at that. When he pulled his gaze from the road ahead, laughter shimmered in his blue eyes.

"No, ma'am. It surely isn't."

Kate didn't reply, but she knew darn well Scott was anything *but* faint of heart. When the air force had identified him as Bill Thompson's replacement, she'd activated her extensive network of friends and information sources to find out everything she could about the man. Her sources confirmed he'd packed a whole bunch of flying time into his ten years in the military.

Flying that included several hundred combat hours in both the Blackhawk helicopter and the AC–130H gunship. A highly modified version of the air force's four-engine turboprop workhorse, the gunship provided surgically accurate firepower in support of both conventional and unconventional forces, day or night.

Kate didn't doubt Scott had provided just that surgically accurate support during recent tours in both Afghanistan and Iraq. After Iraq, he'd been sent to the 919th Special Operations Wing at Hurlburt Field, Florida, to fly the latest addition to the air force inventory—the tilt-wing CV–22 Osprey.

Since the Osprey combined the lift characteristics of a helicopter and the long-distance flight capability of a fixed-wing aircraft, Scott's background made him a natural choice as short-notice replacement for Bill Thompson. If—*when!*—Pegasus completed its operational tests, it might well replace both the C–130 and the CV–122 as the workhorse of the battlefield.

Thinking of the tense weeks ahead, Kate chewed

on her lower lip and said little until they'd passed through the second checkpoint and entered the compound housing the Pegasus test complex.

The entire complex had been sited and constructed in less than two months. Unfortunately, the builders had sacrificed aesthetics to exigency. The site had all the appeal of a prison camp. Rolls of concertina wire surrounded the clump of prefabricated modular buildings and trailers, all painted a uniformly dull tan to blend in with the desert landscape. White-painted rocks marked the roads and walkways between the buildings. Aside from a few picnic tables scattered among the trailers, everything was starkly functional.

Separate modular units housed test operations, the computer-communications center and a dispensary. The security center, nicknamed Rattlesnake Ops after the leather-tough, take-no-prisoners military police guarding the site, occupied another unit. A larger unit contained a fitness center and the dining hall, which also served as movie theater and briefing room when the site's commanding officer wanted to address the entire cadre. The hangar that housed Pegasus loomed over the rest of the structures like a big, brooding mammoth.

Personnel were assigned to the trailers, two or three to a unit. Kate and the other two women officers on-site shared one unit. Scott would bunk down with Major Russ McIver, the senior Marine Corps rep.

Kate directed him to the line of modular units unofficially dubbed Officers Row.

"You probably want to change into your uniform before checking in with Captain Westfall. Your trailer is the second one on the left. Westfall's is the unit standing by itself at the end of the row."

"First things first," Scott countered, pulling up at the small dispensary. "Let's get your ankle looked at."

"I'll take care of that. You'd best get changed and report in."

"Special Ops would drum me out of the brotherhood if I left a lady to hobble around on a sore ankle."

He meant it as a joke, but his careless attitude toward his new assignment was starting to seriously annoy Kate. Her mouth thinned as he came around the front of the pickup. Sliding out of the passenger seat, she stood firmly on both feet to address him.

"I don't think you've grasped the urgency of our mission. I'll manage here, Captain. You report in to the C.O."

Her tone left no doubt. It was an order from a superior officer to a subordinate.

Scott cocked an eyebrow. For a moment, his eyes held something altogether different from the teasing laughter he'd treated her to up to this point.

The dangerous glint was gone almost as quickly

as it had come. Tipping her a two-fingered salute, he replied in an easy, if somewhat exaggerated, drawl.

"Yes, ma'am."

Dave took care not to spin out and leave Lieutenant Commander Hargrave in a swirl of dust. His eyes on the rearview mirror, he followed her careful progress up the clinic steps.

The woman was stubborn as well as gorgeous. And not above pulling rank on him. Well, that pretty well fit with what he'd heard about her.

The sexy Hurricane Hunter couldn't know it but her ex-husband had piloted the mission Dave had flown with the reserve unit out of Keesler. The man had had a few things to say about the wife who'd just dumped him, none of them particularly flattering. She was, according to the still-bitter aviator, ambitious as hell, fearless in the air, a tiger in bed and a real ball-breaker out of it.

Dave figured three out of four was good enough for him.

Yes, sir, he thought as he caught a last glimpse of turquoise spandex in the mirror. This assignment was looking better and better by the minute.

Two

Showered, shaved and wrapped in the familiar comfort of his green Nomex flight suit, Dave tracked down the officer in command of the Pegasus project. He found Captain Westfall at the Test Operations Building.

"Captain Scott reporting for duty, sir."

The tall, lean naval officer in khakis creased to blade-edged precision returned Dave's salute, then offered his hand.

"Welcome aboard, Captain Scott."

The man's gravelly voice and iron grip matched his salt-and-pepper buzz cut. His skin was tanned to near leather, no doubt the result of years spent pacing a deck in sun, wind and salt spray. His piercing gray eyes took deliberate measure of the latest addition to his team. Dave didn't exactly square his shoulders, but he found himself standing a little taller under Westfall's intense scrutiny.

"Did you take care of that bit of personal business you mentioned when you called last night?"

"Yes, sir."

Dave most certainly had. Fighting a grin, he thought of the waitress who'd all but wrapped herself around him when he'd stopped for a cheeseburger in Chorro. The cluster of sunbaked adobe buildings was the closest thing that passed for a town around these parts. The town might appear tired and dusty, but its residents were anything but. One particular resident, anyway.

Dave would carry fond memories of that particular stop for a long time.

Although…

All the while he'd soaped and scraped away the bristles and road dust, his thoughts had centered more on a certain redhead than on the waitress who'd delayed his arrival at the Pegasus site by a few hours. Kate Hargrave was still there, inside his head, teasing him with her fiery hair, her luscious curves and those green cat's eyes.

As if reading his mind, Westfall folded his arms. "I understand you brought Lieutenant Commander Hargrave in this morning."

Word sure got around fast. Dave had dropped off the gorgeous weather officer at the dispensary less than twenty minutes ago.

"Yes, sir. We bumped into each other on the road into the site. Have you had a report on her condition? How's her ankle?"

"Doc Richardson says she'll be fine. Only a slight muscle strain." A flinty smile creased Westfall's cheeks. "Knowing Commander Hargrave, she'll work out the kinks and be back in fighting form within a few hours."

"That's good to hear."

The smile disappeared. Westfall's gray eyes drilled into his new subordinate. "Yes, it is. I can't afford to lose another key member of my test cadre. You've got some catching up to do, Captain."

"Yes, sir."

"I've set up a series of briefings for you, starting at oh-nine-hundred. First, though, I want you to meet the rest of the team. And get a look at the craft you'll be piloting." He flicked a glance at his watch. "I've asked the senior officers and engineers to assemble in the hangar. They should be in place by now."

The hangar was the cleanest Dave had ever seen. No oil spills smudged the gleaming, white-painted floor. No greasy equipment was shoved up against the wall. Just rack after rack of black boxes and the sleek white capsule that was Pegasus. It took everything Dave had to tear his gaze from the delta-winged craft and acknowledge the introductions Captain Westfall performed.

"Since Pegasus is intended for use by all branches of the military, we've pulled together representatives from each of the uniformed services. I understand you've already met Major Russ McIver."

"Right."

The square-jawed marine had just been exiting his trailer when Dave pulled up. They'd exchanged little more than a quick handshake before Dave hurried in to hit the showers and pull on his uniform. From the package headquarters had sent him, though, he knew McIver had proven himself in both Kosovo and Kabul. The marine's function was to test Pegasus's capability as a vehicle for inserting a fully armed strike team deep into enemy territory.

"This is Major Jill Bradshaw," Westfall announced, "chief of security for the site."

A brown-eyed blonde in desert fatigues and an armband with MP stenciled in big white letters, the major held out her hand. "Good to have you on board, Captain. Come by Rattlesnake Ops after the briefing and we'll get you officially cleared in."

"Will do."

The petite brunette next to Bradshaw smiled a welcome. "Lieutenant Caroline Dunn, Coast Guard. Welcome to Project Pegasus, Captain Scott."

"Thanks."

Dave liked her on the spot. From what he'd read of the woman's résumé, she'd racked up an impressive number of hours in command of a Coast Guard cutter. He appreciated both her experience and her warm smile.

"Dr. Cody Richardson," Westfall said next, indicating a tall, black-haired officer in khakis. The silver oak leaf on Richardson's left collar tab designated his rank. On the right tab was the insignia of the Public Health Service—an anchor with a chain fouling it.

A world-renowned expert in biological agents, Richardson held both an M.D. and a Ph.D. His mission was to test the nuclear, biological and chemical defense suite installed in Pegasus. He also served as on-site physician.

"Heard you provided ambulance service this morning," the doc commented, taking Dave's hand in a firm, no-nonsense grip.

"I did. How's your patient?"

His patient answered for herself. Stepping forward, Lieutenant Commander Hargrave gave Dave a cool smile.

"Fit for duty and ready to get to work."

He sure couldn't argue with the "fit" part. Damned if he'd ever seen anyone fill out a flight suit the way Kate Hargrave did. She, too, wore fire-retardant Nomex, but hers was the NOAA version—sky blue instead of the military's pea green. The zippered, one-piece bag sported an American flag on the left shoulder, a leather name patch above her left breast and NOAA's patch above her right. A distinctive unit emblem was Velcroed to her right shoulder.

It featured a winged stallion on a classic shield-shaped device. The bottom two-thirds of the shield was red. The top third showed a blue field studded with seven silver stars. Captain Westfall saw Dave eyeing the patch and reached into his pocket.

"This is for you. I issued one to the entire test cadre when we first assembled. The winged steed speaks for itself. The stars represent each of the seven uniformed services."

Dave's glance swept the assembled group once more. They were all there, all seven. Army. Navy. Marine Corps. Air Force. Coast Guard. Public Health Service. And NOAA, as represented by the delectable Kate Hargrave. The four military branches. Three predominately civilian agencies with small cadres of uniformed officers.

Dave had been assigned to some joint and unified commands before, but never one with this diversity. Despite their variations in mission and uniform, though, each of these officers had sworn the same oath when they were commissioned. To protect and defend the Constitution of the United States against all enemies.

Dave might possess a laid-back attitude toward life

in general, but he took that oath very seriously. No one who'd served in combat could do otherwise.

Captain Westfall took a few moments more to introduce the project's senior civilian scientists and engineers. That done, he and the entire group walked Dave over to the vehicle they'd gathered to test and—hopefully!—clear for operational use.

Pegasus was as sweet up close as it had looked from across the hangar. Long, cigar-shaped, with a bubble canopy, a side hatch and fat, wide-tracked wheels. Designed to operate on land, in the air and in water. The gray-haired Captain Westfall stroked the gleaming white fuselage with the same air of proud propriety a horse breeder might give the winner of the Triple Crown.

"You're seeing the craft in its swept-wing mode," he intoned in his deep voice.

Dave nodded, noting the propellers were folded flat, the engines tilted to horizontal, and the wings tucked almost all the way into the belly of the craft.

"The wide-track wheels allow Pegasus to operate on land in this mode."

"And damned well, too," Dr. Richardson put in with a quick glance at the trim blond Major Bradshaw.

"We encountered some unexpected difficulties during the mountain phase of land operations," she told Dave. "You know about the virus that hit the site and affected Bill Thompson's heart. It hit me, too, while I was up in the mountains conducting a prerun check. Cody… Dr. Richardson and Major McIver rode Pegasus to the rescue.''

She'd corrected her slip into informality quickly, but not before Dave caught the glance she and the doc exchanged. Well, well. So it wasn't all work and no play on the site after all.

"Glad to hear Pegasus can run," Dave commented. "The real test will be to see if he can fly."

He saw at once he'd put his foot in it. Backs stiffened. Eyes went cool. Even Caroline Dunn, the friendly Coast Guard officer, arched an eyebrow.

"Pegasus is designed as a multiservice, all-weather, all-terrain assault vehicle," Captain Westfall reminded him. "Our job is to make sure it operates equally well on land, on water *and* in the air."

There was only one answer to that. Dave gave it. "Yes, sir."

He recovered a little as the walk-around continued and the talk turned to the specifics of the craft's power, torque, engine thrust and instrumentation. Dave had done his homework, knew exactly what was required to launch Pegasus into the air. By the end of the briefing, his hands were itching to wrap around the throttles.

The rest of the day was taken up with the administrivia necessary in any new assignment. Major Bradshaw gave Dave a security briefing and issued a high-tech ID that not only cleared him into the site but also tracked his every movement. Doc Richardson conducted an intake interview and medical assessment. The senior test engineers presented detailed briefings of Pegasus's performance during the land tests.

By the time 7:00 p.m. rolled around, Dave's stomach was issuing noisy feed-me demands. The sandwich he and the briefers had grabbed for lunch had long since ceased to satisfy the needs of his six-two frame. He caught the tail end of the line at the dining hall and joined a table of troops in desert fatigues.

Like the officer cadre, enlisted personnel at the site came from every branch of the service. Army MPs provided security. Navy personnel operated most of the support facilities. Air force troops maintained the site's extensive communications and computer networks. The marine contingent was small, Dave learned, only about ten noncoms whose expertise was essential in testing Pegasus's performance as a troop transport and forward-insertion vehicle.

He scarfed down a surprisingly delicious concoction of steak and enchiladas, then returned to the unit he shared with Russ McIver to unpack and stow his gear. McIver wasn't in residence and the unpacking didn't take long. All Dave had brought with him was an extra flight suit, a set of blues on the off chance he'd have to attend some official function away from the site, workout sweats, jeans, some comfortable shirts and one pair of dress slacks. His golf shoes and clubs he left in the truck. With any luck, he'd get Pegasus soaring the first time up and have time to hit some of New Mexico's golf courses before heading back to his home base in Florida.

Changing out of his uniform into jeans and a gray USAF sweatshirt with the arms ripped out, he stashed his carryall under his bed and explored the rest of the two-bedroom unit. It was similar to a dozen others he'd occupied at forward bases and a whole lot more comfortable than his quarters in Afghanistan.

A passing glance showed Russ McIver's room was spartan in its neat orderliness. As was the front room. Carpeted in an uninspiring green, the area served as a combination eating, dining and living room. The furniture was new and looked comfortable, if not particularly elegant. The fridge was stocked with two boxes of high-nutrition health bars and four six-packs of Coors Light.

"That's what I admire most about marines," Dave announced to the empty trailer. "They take only the absolute necessities into the field with them."

Helping himself, he popped a top and prepared to attack the stack of briefing books and technical manuals he'd plopped down on the kitchenette counter. The rise and fall of voices just outside the unit drew him to the door.

When he stepped out into the early-evening dusk, the first thing that hit him was the explosion of color to the west. Like a smack to the face, it grabbed his instant attention. Reds, golds, blacks, pinks, oranges and blues, all swirling together in a deep purple sky. The gaudy combination reminded Dave of the paintings he'd seen in every truck stop and roadside gift shop on the drive out. Black velvet and bright slashes of color. But this painting was for real, and it was awesome.

The second thing that hit him was the silence his appearance had generated among the officers clustered around a metal picnic table. It was as if an outsider had crashed an exclusive, members-only party. Which he had, Dave thought wryly.

His new roommate broke the small silence. Lifting an arm, McIver waved him over. "Hey, Scott. Bring your beer and join us."

"Thanks." Puffs of sand swirled under Dave's feet as he crossed to the table. "It's your beer, by the way. I'll contribute to the fund or restock the refrigerator as necessary."

"No problem."

The others shifted to make room for him. Like Dave, they'd shed their uniforms. Most wore cutoffs or jeans. Kate Hargrave, he noted with a suddenly dry throat, was in spandex again. Biker shorts this time. Black. Showing lots of slim, tanned thigh.

Damn!

"We were just talking about you," she said as he claimed a corner of the metal bench.

No kidding. He hadn't been hit with a silence like that since the last time he'd walked in on his brother and sister-in-law in the middle of one of the fierce arguments they pretended never happened. As always, Jacqueline had clammed up tight in the presence of a third party. Ryan had just looked angry and miserable. As always.

Jaci was a lot like Kate Hargrave, Dave decided. Not as beautiful. Certainly not as well educated. But just as tough and *very* good at putting a man in his place. Or trying to.

"Must have been a boring conversation," he returned, stretching his legs out under the table. "I'm not much to talk about."

"We were speculating how long it's going to take you to get up to speed."

"I'll be ready to fly when Pegasus is."

Kate arched a delicately penciled auburn eyebrow. "The first flight was originally scheduled for next week. After Bill's heart attack, Captain Westfall put it on hold."

"I talked to him late this afternoon. He's going to put the flight back on as scheduled."

The nonchalant announcement produced another startled silence. Cody Richardson broke it this time.

"Are you sure you can complete your simulator training and conduct the necessary preflight test runs by next week, Scott?"

Dave started to reply that he intended to give it

the ole college try. Just in time, he bit back the laconic quip. It didn't take a genius to see that this gathering under the stars was some kind of nightly ritual. And that Dave was still the odd man out. He'd remain out until he proved himself. Problem was, he'd long ago passed the point of either wanting or needing to prove anything. His record spoke for him.

"Yeah," he answered the doc instead. "I'm sure."

The talk turned to the machine then, the one that had brought them all to this corner of the desert. Dave said little, preferring to listen and add to his first impressions of the group.

There were definitely some personalities at work here, he decided after a few moments of lively discussion. Caroline Dunn, the Coast Guard officer, looked as if a stiff wind could blow her away, but her small form housed a sharp mind and an iron will. That became evident when Russ McIver made the mistake of suggesting some modifications to the sea trials. Dunn cut his feet right out from under him.

Then there was the site's top cop, Army Major Jill Bradshaw. Out of uniform, she lost some of her cool, don't-mess-with-me aura. Particularly around the doc, Dave noted with interest. Yep, those two most certainly had something cooking.

Which left Kissable Kate. Dave would be a long time getting to sleep tonight. The weather scientist did things to spandex that made a man ache to peel off every inch of the slick, rubbery fabric. Slowly. Inch by delicious inch.

So he didn't exactly rush off when the small gathering broke up and the others drifted away, leaving him and Kate and a sky full of stars. Dave retained his comfortable slouch while she played with her diet-drink can and eyed him thoughtfully across the dented metal tabletop.

Light from the high-intensity spots mounted around the compound gave her hair a dark copper tint. She'd caught it back with a plastic clip, but enough loose tendrils escaped for Dave to weave an erotic fantasy or two before she shoved her drink can aside.

"Look, we may have gotten off to a wrong start this morning."

"Can't agree with you on that one," he countered. "Scooping a beautiful woman into my arms ten seconds after laying eyes on her constitutes one heck of a good start in my mind."

"That's exactly what I mean. I don't want you to make the mistake of thinking you'll be scooping me up again."

"Why not?"

The lazy amusement in his voice put an edge in hers.

"I made a few calls. Talked to some people who know you. Does the name Denise Hazleton strike a bell?"

"Should it?"

"No, I guess not. Denise said you never quite got around to last names and probably wouldn't remember her first. She's a lieutenant stationed at Luke Air Force Base, in Arizona. You were hitting on her girlfriend the night the two of you hooked up."

"Hmm. Hooking up with one woman while hitting on another. Not good, huh?"

"Not in my book."

Kate hadn't really expected him to show remorse or guilt. She wouldn't have believed him if he had. But neither was she prepared for the hopeful gleam that sprang into his eyes.

"Did I get lucky with either?"

Well, at least he was honest. The man didn't make any attempt to disguise his nature. He was what he was.

"Yes, you did," she answered. "Which is why..."

"What else did she say?"

"I beg your pardon?"

"Denise. What else did she tell you?"

A bunch! Interspersed with long, breathy sighs and a fervent hope that Captain Dave Scott would find his way back to Luke soon.

"Let's just say you left her with a smile on her face."

"We aim to please," Scott said solemnly, even as

the glint in his blue eyes deepened. Too late, Kate realized he'd been stringing her along.

"The point is," she said firmly, "I was married to a man a lot like you. A helluva pilot, but too handsome for his own—or anyone else's—good. It didn't work for us and I want you to know right up-front I've sworn off the type."

One sun-bleached eyebrow hooked. He studied Kate for long moments. "That flight I told you about? The one I took a year or so ago with the air force Hurricane Hunters out of Keesler?"

"Yes?"

"Your ex-husband was the pilot."

Kate's mouth twisted. Obviously she wasn't the only one who got an earful. "You don't have to tell me. I'll just assume John implied I didn't leave *him* with a smile on his face."

"Something along those lines."

She cocked her head, curious now about the workings of this man's mind. "And that didn't scare you off?"

His grin came back, swift and slashing and all male. "No, ma'am."

"It should have. As I said, it didn't work out between John and me. Just as it wouldn't work between the two of us."

"Well, I'm not looking for a deep, meaningful relationship, you understand...."

"Somehow I didn't think you were," Kate drawled.

"But that's not to say we couldn't test the waters."

"No, thanks."

She scooted off the end of the bench and rose. She'd said what needed saying. The conversation was finished.

Evidently Scott didn't agree. Uncoiling his long frame from the opposite bench, he came around to her side of the table.

"You're a scientist. You tote a Ph.D. after your name. I would think you'd want to conduct a series of empirical tests and collect some irrefutable data before you write us off."

"I've collected all the data I need."

"Denise might not agree."

There it was again. That glint of wicked laughter.

"I'm sure she wouldn't," Kate agreed.

"Then I'd say you owe it to yourself to perform at least one definitive test."

His hand came up, curled under her chin, tipped her face. Kate knew she could stop this with a single word. She hadn't reached the rank of lieutenant commander in NOAA's small commissioned-officer corps without learning how to handle herself in just about any situation.

She could only blame curiosity—and the determination to show Dave Scott she meant business—for the way she stood passive and allowed him to conduct the experiment.

Three

———

He knew how to kiss. Kate would give him that.

He didn't swoop. Didn't zero in hard and fast. He took things slow, easy, his mouth playing with hers, his breath a warm wash against her lips. Just tantalizing enough to stir small flickers of pleasure under her skin. Just teasing enough to make her want more.

Sternly, Kate resisted the urge to tilt her head and make mouth more accessible. Not that Scott required her assistance. His thumb traced a slow circle on the underside of her chin and gently nudged it to a more convenient angle for his greater height. By the time the experiment ended, Kate was forced to admit the truth.

"That was nice."

"Nice, huh?"

"Very nice," she conceded. "But it didn't light any fires."

Not major ones, anyway. Just those irritating little flickers still zapping along her nerve endings.

"That was only an engine check." His thumb made another lazy circle on the underside of her chin. "Next time, we'll rev up to full throttle."

It wouldn't do any good to state bluntly there wouldn't be a next time. Dave Scott would only take that as another personal challenge.

"Tell you what." Deliberately, she eased away from his touch. "I'll let you know when I'm ready to rev my engines. Until then, we focus only on our mission while on-site. Agreed?"

"If that's what you want."

She leveled a steady look at him. Ignored the little crinkle of laugh lines at the corners of his eyes. Disregarded the way the deepening shadows cast his face into intriguing planes and angles.

"That's what I want."

Kate had almost as much trouble convincing her roommates she wanted to stick strictly to business as she had convincing Dave Scott.

Cari and Jill were both waiting when she returned to the modular unit that served as their quarters. The unit was functional at best—three cracker box–size bedrooms, an even smaller kitchen and a living area equipped with furniture more designed for utility than for comfort. The three women had added a few personal touches. Kate had tacked up some posters showing the earth's weather in all its infinite variety. Cloudbursts over the Grand Canyon. Snow dusting the peaks of the Andes. The sun blazing down on a Swiss alpine meadow. Cari had added a shelf crammed with the whodunits and thrillers she devoured like candy. Jill stuck to her army roots and had draped a green flag depicting the crossed dueling pistols of the Military Police over one bare wall. The result wouldn't win any house-beautiful awards, but the three officers had grown used to it.

They'd also grown used to each other's idiosyncrasies. No small feat for women accustomed to being on their own and in charge. Still, their close quarters made for few secrets—as Cari proceeded to demonstrate. Curled in her favorite chair, the Coast Guard officer propped the thick technical manual she'd been studying on her chest and demanded an account.

"Okay, Hargrave, *re-port.* What's with you and the latest addition to our merry band?"

"Other than the fact he drove me into the compound after my tumble this morning, nothing."

Polite disbelief skipped across Cari's heart-shaped face. Jill Bradshaw was more direct.

"Ha! Some weather officer you are. *We* all heard

the thunder rumbling around you and Scott. You sure lightning isn't about to strike?''

''I should be so lucky.''

Kate plopped down beside her on the sofa and yanked the clip out of her hair. Raking her fingers through the heavy mass, she gave the cop a rueful smile.

''I'll tell you this much. Dave isn't like Cody, Jill. You struck gold there.''

''Yeah, right,'' the blonde snorted. ''I had to put him on his face in the dirt before either of us got around to recognizing that fact. Not to mention almost arresting him for suspected sabotage.''

Kate's smile dimmed at the memory of those tense days when a mysterious virus had attacked one team member after another. As chief of security, Jill's investigation had centered on the Public Service officer—who just happened to be one of the country's foremost experts in biological agents.

''Besides which,'' Jill continued with a shrug, ''Cody and I are doing our best to play things cool until we wind up the Pegasus project.''

It was Kate's turn to snort. ''The temperature goes up a good twenty degrees Celsius whenever you two are in the same vicinity.''

Loftily, her roommate ignored the interruption. ''From where we sit,'' Jill said, including Cari in the general assessment, ''your Captain Scott doesn't look like he knows how to cool his jets.''

"First, he's not *my* Captain Scott. Second, we conducted a little experiment a few moments ago, the nature of which is highly classified," she added firmly when both women flashed interested looks. "Bottom line, the captain and I agreed to focus solely on Pegasus while on-site. As the three of us should be doing right now."

Jill took the hint and stopped probing. An intensely private person herself, she hadn't looked forward to sharing cramped quarters with two other women. After weeks with the gregarious Kate and friendly Caroline, she'd learned to open up a bit. Falling head over heels for the handsome doc assigned to the project had certainly aided in her metamorphosis.

"Speaking of Pegasus," Cari said, patting the thick three-ring binder propped on her stomach. "Captain Westfall sent over a revised test plan while you were out, uh, experimenting with Dave Scott. Our air force flyboy starts simulator training tomorrow morning."

"Yikes!" Kate's feet hit the floor with a thud. "I'd better get to work. I want to input a different weather-sequence pattern into the simulator program. Talk to you guys later."

Heading for her bedroom, she settled at the small desk wedged in a corner and flipped up the lid of a slim, titanium-cased notebook computer. The communications wizards assigned to the Pegasus project had rigged wireless high-speed satellite links for the

PCs on-site. Kate could access the National Ocean-ographic and Atmospheric Agency databases from just about anywhere in the compound.

The databases were treasure troves containing information collected over several centuries. Kate took pride in the fact that NOAA could trace its roots back to 1807, when President Thomas Jefferson created the U.S. Coast and Geodetic Survey, the oldest scientific agency in the federal government. Congress got involved in 1890 when it created a Weather Bureau, the forerunner of the current National Weather Service. In 1970 President Nixon combined weather and coastal surveys, along with many other departments to create NOAA.

The major component of the Department of Commerce, NOAA had responsibilities that now included all U.S. weather and climate forecasting, monitoring ocean and atmospheric data, managing marine fisheries and mammals, mapping and charting all U.S. waters and managing coastal zones. Counted among its vast resources were U.S. weather and environmental satellites, a fleet of ships and aircraft, twelve research laboratories and several supercomputers.

Civilians constituted most of NOAA's personnel, but a small cadre of uniformed officers served within all components of the agency, as well as with the military services, NASA, the Department of State and the new Department of Homeland Security. A privileged few like Kate got to fly with the Hurricane

Hunters based out of the Aviations Operations Center in Tampa.

Kate hadn't intended to join NOAA or its officer corps, had never *heard* of the agency when she started working part-time in a TV station while still in high school. Before long, she was helping analyze data and put together weather reports. She didn't seriously consider a career in weather, though, until Hurricane Andrew devastated her grandparents' retirement community just outside Miami. She spent weeks helping the heartbroken couple sort through the soggy remains of fifty-two years of marriage. The experience gave her keen insight into the way natural disasters impacted people's lives.

After that wrenching experience, weather became not just a part-time job, but a passion. Kate majored in meteorology in college, served an internship with the National Weather Service's Tornado Center in Oklahoma, went on to earn a master's and then a doctorate in environmental sciences. Now one of the senior scientists assigned to NOAA's Air Operations Center, Kate regularly devoured materials on everything from tidal waves to meteor showers.

Captain Westfall had handpicked Kate for the Pegasus project based on her expertise and her reputation within the agency for always producing results. Pegasus wasn't designed to fly or swim through hurricanes, but it was expected to operate on land, in the air and at sea. Kate had drawn on NOAA's extensive databases to design tests that would stress the vehicle's instrumentation and its crew to the max in each environment.

For the land runs, she'd simulated sandstorms, raging blizzards, flood conditions and blistering heat. For the airborne phase of the tests, she planned to subject the craft to an even more drastic assortment of natural phenomena.

Her fingers flew over the keyboard, reviewing the test parameters, adjusting weather-severity levels, adding electronic notes to herself and the senior test engineer who'd have to approve any modifications to the plan.

A final click of the mouse saved the changes. Kate sat back, a small smile on her face.

"Okay, Captain Dave Scott. This little package ought to put you through your paces. You and Pegasus both."

Still smiling, she changed into a well-washed, comfortable sleep shirt. It was early, not quite ten, but she'd have to be up by six to squeeze in her morning run.

Usually Kate zonked out within moments of hitting the sack. Tonight she couldn't seem to erase the image of a certain pilot. Or the memory of his mouth brushing hers. Damn, the man was good! Despite her every intention to the contrary, he'd certainly left her wanting more.

Okay, and what woman wouldn't? Kate rationalized. With his muscled shoulders, gleaming blue eyes and come-and-get-me grin, the man was sex on the hoof. Then there was his attitude. So damned cocky and confident. She had to admire his seemingly unshakable belief in his own abilities, even as she felt a growing urge to take him down a peg or two.

Well, he'd get a chance to show what he was made of tomorrow.

Rolling over, Kate punched her pillow.

Her inner alarm woke her well before six. The clock radio beside her bed went off just as she was lacing her running shoes. Killing the alarm, Kate put on a pot of coffee for her roommates and slipped outside to conduct her warm-up exercises. The muscles she'd pulled yesterday morning issued a sharp protest, but the ache eased within moments. Properly stretched and loose, she set out at an easy lope for the gate guarding the compound.

The MP on duty tipped her a salute. Kate returned it with a smile and lengthened her stride. The dirt road that formed the only access to the site arrowed straight ahead, a pale track in the light filtering through the peaks to the east. The steady plop of her sneakers against the dirt and the rhythm of her own breathing soon took Kate to her special, private world.

Her morning run was a sacred ritual, one she conducted whenever she didn't have a flight scheduled or a hurricane to track. The stillness of early morning cleared her head of yesterday's issues and centered her on the ones ahead. Given her penchant for pizza and greasy cheeseburgers, the long, punishing runs also kept her naturally lush curves from becoming downright generous.

After her divorce, these moments alone in the dawn had helped her regain her perspective. It had taken her a while to get past the hurt. Even longer to recognize that John's angry accusation that Kate was too driven, too ambitious, masked his own unwillingness to abandon the niche he'd carved for himself in his world. He didn't want change—or a wife who thrived on challenges.

With an impatient shake of her head, Kate put the past out of her mind. This was her quiet time, her small slice where she should be thinking about the day ahead.

So she wasn't particularly thrilled when she caught the echo of a loping tread behind her. Most of the other personnel at the test cadre fulfilled their mandatory physical fitness requirements at the site's small but well-equipped gym. Once a week Russ McIver rousted the marine contingent on station for a ten-mile run. With full backpacks, no less. Aside from that grunting, huffing squad, Kate usually had the dawn to herself.

When thuds drew closer, she threw a look over her

shoulder. Dave Scott caught her glance and jerked his chin in acknowledgment.

Well, hell!

An irritated frown creased Kate's forehead. She thought she'd made herself clear last night. Apparently Captain Scott hadn't been listening. Her mouth set, she brought her head back around and kept to her pace.

He came up alongside her a few moments later. "Mornin', Commander. You sure you should be running on that ankle?"

She ignored the question and the easy smile he aimed her way. "I thought we reached an agreement last night."

"We did."

"And this is how you intend to stick to your end of the bargain?"

"Maybe I misunderstood things." He sounded genuinely puzzled as he matched his longer stride to hers. "I thought we agreed to focus on business while on-site."

"Exactly."

"So I'm focusing. Captain Westfall made it clear he expected all military to maintain a vigorous physical-conditioning program."

"And you just happened to choose an early-morning run for your PE program?"

The sarcasm went right past the captain.

"I figured the rest of the day was going to be

pretty busy,'' he replied. "I also figured you might want some company. Just in case you went into a ditch and made contact with another tumbleweed.''

"Sorry, cowboy, you figured wrong. Company is the last thing I want on my morning run. I use the time to clear my head and raise a little sweat.''

"Not a problem,'' he said easily. "I like a little more kick in my stride anyway. I wouldn't want to push you.''

She shook her head. As challenges went, that one was about as subtle as a bull moose pawing the ground.

"If you want a race…''

She skimmed her glance over the desert landscape now bathed in the reds and golds of morning. A half mile or so ahead, a solitary cactus raised its arms as if to welcome the new day.

"See that cactus? If I reach it first, you pick another time to run. Agreed?''

"Agr— Hey!''

She shot forward, feeding off a rush of pure adrenaline. Kate loved pushing herself to the max. In the air, surrounded by a riot of black, angry clouds and howling winds. On the playing field, whether participating or watching. In her personal life, which she had to admit had taken on an unexpected edge since Dave Scott appeared on the scene all of twenty-four hours ago.

Unfortunately, most men didn't appreciate being

left in the dust. Kate had learned that lesson the hard way from her ex. She figured now was as good a time as any to administer the same lesson to Dave Scott.

She almost succeeded. The cool desert air was stabbing into her lungs as she drew level with the cactus. At that moment, Scott drew level with her. They whizzed past the plant side by side, matching stride for stride.

Panting, Kate slowed her breakneck pace. Scott did the same, his breath coming a whole lot easier than hers.

"What do you know?" he said, that damned glint in his eye. "A tie."

"Did you hold back?" she asked sharply.

"What do you think?"

"Dammit, Scott!"

"Hey, you set the ground rules. You win, I run another time. I win, I run when and where I please. A tie…"

"A tie means we do it again," Kate snapped. She didn't like losing *or* ending matters in a draw.

"Okay by me. So how far do you plan to run this morning?"

"Another mile or so," she bit out.

"That works. I need to hit the showers and make a pass through the dining hall before I show up at test ops for my first simulator run."

Kate chewed on her lower lip. A few strides later, she offered a grudging bit of advice.

"You might want to skip the dining hall. You're going to hit some rough weather this morning. You won't impress your fellow cadre members if you up-chuck the first time you're at the controls."

He gave her a quick glance. "Taking me on a wild ride, are you?"

"Like you wouldn't believe, cowboy."

As soon as the words were out, Kate wished them back. She couldn't believe she'd let herself walk into that bit of double entendre. To her surprise, Scott didn't jump on it with wolfish glee. He looked thoughtful for a moment before nodding his thanks.

"I appreciate the warning. I'll go light on the grits and gravy."

"Good idea."

The warning surprised Dave. Given what he'd heard about Kate Hargrave's competitive personality, he would have guessed she'd take secret delight in knocking him down a peg or two. She'd certainly pulled out all the stops in their little footrace a mo-ment ago. Dave had burned more energy than he wanted to admit trying to catch her. Once she got back up to full power she was going to give him one helluva run for his money.

A smile of pure anticipation tugged at his lips. Be-hind his laid-back exterior, Dave was every bit as competitive as Commander Hargrave. He suspected all fliers had that edge, that instinctive need to beat the odds every time they climbed into the cockpit. But it had been a while since he'd felt the thrill of the chase this keenly. Even longer since he'd been shot down in flames.

Kate had all but waved a red flag in front of his face last night by insisting on their so-called agreement. Dave wouldn't break his word. He'd stick to the terms—as he interpreted them. He'd also do his damnedest to convince her to renegotiate their contract.

Dave wasn't quite sure how it had happened, but the challenge represented by Kate Hargrave was starting to rank right up there with that of Pegasus.

Four

The simulator crouched like a giant blue beetle on long, pneumatic legs. The capsule's front faced huge trifold screens. Once the ride began, the screens would show vivid, dizzying projections of earth and sky. Off to one side a control booth housed the simulator's team of operators, evaluators and observers.

Anticipation simmered in Dave's veins as he climbed the metal stairs to the capsule's entrance. This was his first time at the controls of a brand-new flying, fighting vehicle. He couldn't wait to see how it handled in this simulated environment.

A technician in white overalls with the cadre's distinctive red-and-blue patch prominently displayed waited for him on the platform.

"Ready to fly, Captain?"

"Ready as I'll ever be."

The technician grinned. "I've got a six-pack riding on you. Try not to crash and burn first time up."

"I'll do my best."

Ducking through the side hatch, Dave strapped himself into the operator's seat. Pegasus had been designed for one pilot. Driver. Captain. Whatever they called the individual in the front seat, he or she had to know how to switch from land to airborne to sea mode and operate safely in all three environments. No small feat for anyone, even the highly experienced crew assembled here in the desert.

The tech checked the parachute pack built into the seat, adjusted the shoulder straps on Dave's harness and conducted a final communications check. Just before he closed the door, he offered a final bit of advice.

"Your puke 'n' go bag is right next to your left knee. In case you need it."

"Got it."

The door clanged shut, leaving Dave alone in the simulator. He'd spent most of yesterday and a good portion of last night poring over a fat technical manual, reacquainting himself with instrumentation that was familiar, studying the dials and digital displays that weren't.

He dragged out the black notebook containing the various operational checklists, propped it in the slot designed to hold it and studied the layout of the instruments. The simulator cockpit replicated the actual vehicle exactly. The same defense contractor who'd designed and built the three Pegasus prototypes had constructed the simulator.

Unfortunately, two of the three prototypes had crashed and burned during the developmental phase. Only one had survived and been delivered to the military for operational testing. The contractor was scrambling to produce additional test vehicles, but until they were delivered Dave sure as hell had better not crash the one remaining.

For that reason, these hours in the simulator were absolutely vital. Dave had to get a feel for the craft, had to learn to handle it in all possible situations, before he actually took it into the air. He took a last look around and flipped open the black notebook to the sheet containing the start-up checklist.

"Okay, team. Let's roll."

Captain Westfall's voice came through the headset. "Good luck, Scott."

"Thanks, sir."

Suddenly, the tall screens surrounding the front of the capsule came to life. Instead of dull white, they showed a desert landscape of silver greens and browns. Jagged mountains dominated the horizon. A brilliant blue sky beckoned.

Dave's gloved hand hovered over the red power switch. He dragged in a deep breath, let it out.

"Pegasus One, initiating power."

"Roger, Pegasus One."

Flicking the switch to on, Dave listened to the familiar hum of auxiliary power units feeding juice to the on-board systems. Screens lit up. Switches glowed red and green and yellow.

His gaze went to the digital display showing an outline of Pegasus. The craft was in land mode, its wings back and turboprop engines tucked away. In this mode the vehicle could race across the desert and climb mountains. Much as Dave would love to take this baby out for a run, his job was to test its wings.

"Pegasus One switching to airborne mode."

"Roger, One."

His thumb hit the center button beside the display. Right before his eyes, the shape of the vehicle outlined on the screen altered. Wings fanned out. Propeller blades were released from their tucked position. Rear stabilizers unfolded.

"Hot damn!"

"Come again, Captain?" The simulator operator's voice floated through his headset. "We didn't copy that."

"Sorry. That wasn't meant for public consumption. Pegasus One, locking into hover position."

Like the tilt-wing Osprey currently in use by the military, Pegasus incorporated Very Short Takeoff and Landing technology. With the engines in a vertical position, the craft could lift and hover like a chopper. Dave had logged several hundred hours in the Osprey and was feeling more confident by the moment.

"Pegasus One, powering up."

The familiar whine of engines revving filled his ears. The pedals shuddered under his boots. He took the craft to simulated full power and lifted off. Once airborne, he tilted the engines to horizontal. Pegasus seemed to leap to life.

They gave him a good hour to get a feel for the controls and build his confidence before the first system malfunction occurred. It was minor, a glitch in the navigational transponder. Dave corrected by switching from direct-satellite signal to relay-station signal.

A few moments later, his Doppler radar picked up some weather. A thunderstorm, racing right toward him from the west. That was Kate Hargrave's doing, Dave thought with a smile. Unless he missed his guess, he was in for a rough ride.

Sure enough, the turbulence proved too big to go around and too high to get above. Within moments, thunder crashed in his headset and lightning forked across the wide screens surrounding the capsule. Violent winds set Pegasus bucking and kicking like a wild mustang. Dave needed both hands and feet to maintain control. The wild jolting caused another malfunction. A blinking red light signaled an oil leak in engine one.

His pucker factor rising, Dave shut down the engine and fought to keep the craft in the air while diagnosing the source of the leak. He'd just narrowed it down, when a bolt of lightning slashed across the screen. Bright blue light filled the cockpit. A loud alarm sounded at the same instant another red warning light began to flash.

Hell! Number two engine took a hit. The damned thing was on fire.

Gritting his teeth, Dave flipped to the engine fire checklist. He had to restart engine one before shutting down two, though, or he'd fall right out of the sky. He got the starboard engine powered back up again, killed the other and activated the fire-suppression system.

At that point, the situation went from bad to downright ugly. The damned fire-suppression system didn't work. If anything, the fire appeared to be burning hotter, and electrical systems were shutting down faster than small-town storefronts on a Saturday night.

Too late, Dave remembered the pylons securing the engines to the wing were made of a magnesium alloy. The alloy was strong, light and flexible—all highly desirable qualities in an aircraft. But when magnesium burned, it produced its own oxygen and thus created a fire that was totally self-sustaining.

Chances were this one would eat right through the wing and hit the fuel lines.

In any other aircraft, the pilot would bail out at this point. Dave was damned if he'd punch and lose the only Pegasus prototype left, even in a simulated situation. Sweating inside his flight suit, he tried every trick in the book and a few that had never been written down to save his craft. He was still fighting when his instrument panel went dead.

"Pegasus One, your flight is terminated."

Cursing under his breath, Dave slumped back in the seat and waited for his heart to stop jackhammering against his ribs. He glanced to his right, saw a grim-faced Captain Westfall standing behind the controller in the operator's booth. Kate was next to him, her hair a bright flame in the dimly lit booth. The other officers ringed her.

His mouth set into a hard, tight line, Dave keyed his mike. "Let's conduct the postflight critique. Then we'll try this little exercise again."

In the next two days Dave battled everything from wind shears and microbursts to turbulence that almost flipped over his craft and maintenance-generated crossed wires that caused his instruments to produce faulty readings.

On one flight, he lost cabin pressurization and discovered his oxygen mask wouldn't filter the carbon monoxide he exhaled. On another, an engine stuck halfway between the vertical and horizontal position. He almost crawled out of the simulator after that particular exercise. Both arms and legs ached from using brute physical strength to wrestle with the controls of the wildly gyrating vehicle.

As a result, he wasn't in the mood for another critique of his flying skills when he joined Kate for a run the morning after that particular experience.

She'd come to accept his company with resignation if not an abundance of enthusiasm. Impatient, she paced the dirt just outside his trailer. Her hair was caught up in a ponytail, her body encased in slick-looking hot pink. Dave's stiff movements as he exited his quarters had her quirking an auburn eyebrow.

"Sure you want to run this morning?"

"Yeah."

"Better not overdo it. That last ride was a bitch."

"I was there, remember?"

His curt tone arched her eyebrow another notch. "Suit yourself."

Propping her foot on a rock, she stretched her calf muscles. The sight of all that hot pink bending and curving didn't help Dave's mood. He'd spent the past couple of nights mentally reviewing each phase of every simulated flight. When his mind wasn't churning over the effects of wing icing and emergency high-altitude landings, his thoughts had a distinct tendency to veer off in a direction that left him in even more of a sweat.

He'd replayed the kiss he and Kate had shared a dozen or more times in his mind, kicking himself each time for wimping it. He'd promised her the next one would *not* be slow and easy, and he was ready to deliver on his promise. More than ready.

Cursing himself for agreeing to her hands-off on-site policy, Dave cut his stretching exercise short.

"You ready?"

"Ready."

Kate set off at an easy pace. She'd spent enough time in this man's company by now to gauge his temper. For three days he'd been battling a machine and everything the test cadre had thrown at him. He'd won most of the battles, more than anyone had expected him to. But the ones he'd lost stuck in his craw like a fish bone.

He needed an outlet for his frustration and Kate intended to give him one. Not the one he'd no doubt prefer, she thought with a twinge of real regret. No hard, fast tussle between the sheets, muscles straining, bodies writhing, skin damp with sweat. Gulping at the image that leaped into her head, she kicked up the pace.

Dave lengthened his stride and kept up with her. He didn't indulge in his usual teasing banter. To Kate's surprise, she found she missed the give-and-take. They jogged in silence a while longer before she dropped the casual challenge.

"There's the cactus we used as a finish line the other day," she said. "We talked about a rematch. You up for it?"

He shot her a quick, hard glance. "Are you?"

In answer she merely smiled and took off in a burst of speed.

"Dammit!"

His curse was followed by the sound of his pounding footsteps. Kate didn't hold back. Fists clenched, feet pumping, heart galloping, she poured everything she had into the all-for-nothing sprint.

Mere yards from the cactus she glanced over her shoulder and debated whether to slow her pace. Her goal was to make Dave work off some of his pent-up frustration, not add to it with another defeat. The issue became moot, though, when he laid on a final burst of speed. It was all Kate could do to stay elbow-to-elbow with him as they sailed past the spiky cactus.

Grinning, she slowed her pace. "Well, what do you know," she panted. "Another tie."

"Only because you cheated. Again."

His scowl was gone, replaced by an answering grin that snatched what little air Kate had managed to draw into her already stressed lungs.

"You won't get the drop on me again," he warned.

"Think so, huh? Wait till you climb back in the simulator this morning. You're not going to know what hit you."

His groan was loud and long, but minus the surly edge. "I've already been hit with lightning, hail, ice and sandstorms. What the heck have you got left in your bag of tricks to throw at me?"

She tossed her head, laughing. "Oh, cowboy, I'm just warming up."

"I'll remember this. Trust me, I'm going to re-member every jolt and lurch and sickening, thousand-foot drop."

"Ha! Threats don't scare me."

"They should." His voice dropped to a mock growl. "You're gonna pay, babe."

The promise hovered between them for an endless moment before being lost to the steady plop of their running shoes against the dirt road.

Their race might have relieved some of Dave's frustration, but it didn't help the tension that crawled up Kate's neck as the rest of the day turned into a replay of the ones that had gone before.

They put the sky jock through hell. Time and time again. Using a dial-a-disaster approach, they'd start with a minor problem like an electrical failure, then pile on problem after problem until Dave reached the point of what was politely referred to as task satu-ration. With six or seven major malfunctions occurring at once, he had to scramble to keep the issues sorted out and Pegasus in the air.

By the third simulated run, Kate was sweating under her flight suit and strung tight with nerves. This run would be the worst, she knew. It was an overland flight in winter weather conditions. Partway into the flight, Dave would encounter a phenomenon few pilots had ever dealt with. Swallowing, Kate glanced at the digital clock on the controller's console. Seven minutes until all hell broke loose.

Fists balled, she kept her eyes glued to the wide screens surrounding the capsule. The Alps rose in majestic splendor. Their snowcapped peaks speared into a dazzlingly blue sky. Dave was piloting his craft through a narrow valley. All systems were fully functioning.

Kate tore her gaze from the screens and watched the clock. Three minutes. Two.

She closed her eyes. Envisioned the cold, dense air mass sliding down the mountain. Picking up speed as gravity took over. Sweeping up snow. Gathering force and fury.

"What the…!"

Suddenly Dave was fighting for control in total whiteout conditions. The katabatic wind—the strongest on the planet save for tornadoes—had hit his craft with the force of a free-falling bulldozer. In the Antarctic, these dense, cold down drafts had been clocked at speeds in excess of two hundred miles per hour. In the Alps they came with the mistral, which tore down the Rhone valley through southern France and out into the Mediterranean.

Kate had intensified this particular mistral beyond what might reasonably be expected, given the simulated time of year and temperature. Now she watched with her heart in her throat as the display screens in the control booth showed a snow-blinded, out-of-control Pegasus flying straight at a towering peak.

Pull up! The silent prayer intensified to a near shriek inside her head. *Pull up!*

For a heart-stopping moment, she thought he'd make it. He yanked on the stick, got the craft's nose up, almost—*almost!*—maneuvered around the towering wall of snow and rock.

A second later, the displays went flat. The controller blew out a long, ragged breath and keyed his mike.

"Pegasus One, your flight is terminated."

A stark silence descended over the control booth. Russ McIver finally broke it. "That's twice Scott has augered in now."

His eyes flinty, Captain Westfall nodded. "I'm aware of that, Major."

"I don't think we can blame this one on pilot error or unfamiliarity with the systems," Kate said carefully. "I may have made the weather conditions too extreme for this scenario."

Russ set his jaw. "Extreme or not, if this had been

a real mission we'd be calling for body bags right now.''

As frustrated as everyone else in the booth, Cari Dunn dragged off her ball cap and raked a hand through her hair. "Why don't you wait for the debrief before you start burying the dead, McIver."

The marine stiffened up. "Are you addressing me, *Lieutenant?*"

"Yes, *Major,*" she snapped. "I am."

Dave's voice came over the intercom, cutting through the tension with the precision of a blade.

"Russ is right. I blew it. Let's run this one again."

Captain Westfall leaned into the mike. "You've been at this twelve solid hours. Why don't you take a break and we'll run it tomorrow."

"I'm okay, sir. I'll take another stab at it. What the hell hit me, anyway?"

All eyes in the booth turned to Kate. She stepped up to the mike.

"It's called a katabatic wind, after the Greek word *kata,* meaning downward. It forms when a cold, dense mass of air slides down a mountainside, picks up speed and plunges to the valley below. This type of wind occurs everywhere on the planet but, uh, not usually with this much force."

She half expected him to mutter an angry curse. Kate knew she wouldn't be feeling too friendly if someone had just put her through that particular experience. To her surprise, a chuckle floated across the speakers.

"Don't forget, Hargrave. I'm keeping score. Every lurch. Every jolt. Every damned kata-whatever. Okay, team, let's power this baby up and see if I can get Pegasus to ride on the wind this time."

Five

The officers didn't gather at the picnic tables that night. Or the next. Dave kept them at the simulator, conducting run after run, analyzing the system failures, admitting his own with brutal honesty.

By Friday the entire test cadre was worn to the bone, but both Dave and Pegasus had proved their stuff. In simulated environments, anyway. The real test would come with the first actual flight on Monday morning.

Dave had planned to spend the weekend prepping for the flight, but Captain Westfall gathered his officers and senior civilians early Saturday to declare a stand-down.

"I received a request from the Joint Chiefs for a briefing on our progress to date. I'm flying to Washington this morning and will return Sunday evening. We'll resume test operations on Monday."

His glance roamed from one to another of his senior officers and civilians. The strain of the past weeks showed clearly in their faces.

"Use this downtime to give your troops a break. You folks take one, too. I want everyone rested, relaxed and ready to launch Pegasus into the sky by oh-seven-hundred Monday morning."

He didn't get any arguments. Dave noted how Doc Richardson's glance skipped immediately to Jill Bradshaw. The blonde kept her expression deliberately neutral, but a slight flush rose in her cheeks. Dave would bet his last buck those two would have headed for the nearest motel as soon as this meeting broke up if not for the fact that Richardson stood next in order of rank.

"Commander Richardson has the stick until I return," Westfall said, confirming the doc's seniority. "He'll have to remain on-site during my absence, but the rest of you are free to take off."

"I haven't been off-site since I arrived," Russ McIver commented as the small group walked out into the bright morning sunlight. "I'll have to figure out what to do with myself."

"How about we hit the links?" Dave suggested.

"I've got my golf clubs stashed in my truck. I hear Fort Bliss has a great course."

"Sorry, never had time to learn the game."

Cari couldn't resist. "Too busy polishing your combat boots?"

Mac's eyes narrowed. "My boots aren't the only articles that need polishing around here, Lieutenant. Your attitude could use a little work."

"Is that right?" The Coast Guard officer smiled politely. "Are you going to put me in a brace and work on my military manners?"

The marine gave her a long, considering look. "If I put you in a brace," he said finally, "your manners wouldn't be all we worked on."

Cari's smile slipped. Before she could decide just how to respond, Mac tipped two fingers in a casual salute and strode off. Frowning, the brunette watched him disappear around a corner before she spun on her heel and headed in the opposite direction.

"Well," Kate murmured when the dust settled. "That was interesting."

"Very," Jill Bradshaw agreed. The cop slanted a glance at Cody Richardson, and Dave guessed it wouldn't be long before the two of them disappeared as well. The doc couldn't leave the site, but this was a *big* site, with lots of long, empty stretches of road.

Dave guessed right. Not ten seconds later Jill said she needed to run a perimeter check and Cody volunteered to run it with her. That left Kate, who surprised Dave by falling in with his original suggestion.

"I've knocked around a few white balls in my time. I wouldn't mind getting off-site for a few hours to find out if I've still got my swing."

She still had it. It was right there, in every long-legged stride. Dave could vouch for that.

"What kind of handicap do you carry?" he asked, wondering if she was as good at golf as she seemed to be at everything else.

"Seven."

Well, that answered that.

"What's yours?"

"Twelve."

Her mouth curved in a smug smile. "Looks like I'll have to give you some strokes, cowboy."

With a silent groan, Dave passed on that one.

"Of course," she continued, her competitive batteries already charging, "we'll have to adjust for the fact that you'll be using your own clubs and I'll have to make do with rentals."

"Of course."

"And I'll be in sneakers instead of golf shoes."

"Mine are soft spiked," Dave protested.

"Doesn't matter. They still give you a better grip on the turf."

"All right, already. We'll negotiate the handicaps when we get there. I'll pick you up in twenty minutes."

Thinking that this week from hell just might end a whole lot more enjoyably than he would have imagined a few hours ago, Dave peeled off and headed for his trailer to change out of his uniform and into civvies.

Kate couldn't believe the weight that rolled off her shoulders as Dave's battered pickup passed through the perimeter checkpoint. She loved working on the Pegasus project, was thrilled to have been chosen as the NOAA rep. Still, she hadn't realized how the weeks of excitement and pressure had accumulated until the pickup hit the county road. With that transition from packed dirt to pavement, she felt as though she was reentering the world.

Sighing, Kate slouched down in her seat. Desert landscape rolled by outside the pickup. Inside, the lively strains of Trisha Yearwood's latest hit rolled from the radio.

"Captain Westfall was right," she commented as the song ended. "We needed to stand down and give folks a break. I can't believe how good it feels to get off-site for a few hours."

Dave nodded, but didn't comment. As the newest member of the group, Kate supposed he could hardly complain about the stress. Not that the entire cadre hadn't done their best to pile it on him this week.

If all those hours in the simulator had gotten to him, it didn't show in his face or lazy slouch. Like

Kate, he'd changed into comfortable slacks and a knit shirt. The short-sleeved shirt was collared, as required by many golf courses, and looked as though Ralph Lauren had designed it with him in mind. The cobalt color deepened the blue of his eyes and contrasted vividly with his tanned skin and tawny hair. Kate was still secretly admiring the way the knit stretched across his muscled shoulders when they passed through the small town of Chorro.

A few miles beyond the town, Dave pulled up at an intersection. The two-lane county road they were traveling wound through the desert. To the west, it led to Las Cruces. To the east, to El Paso and the army post at Fort Bliss. The road intersecting it ran north toward Alamogordo and south to God knew where in Mexico.

Dave hooked his wrists over the steering wheel and angled Kate a considering glance. She couldn't tell what he was thinking, but it was clear he had some change of plan in mind.

"Why the stop?" she asked.

"I'm thinking we might extend this excursion for more than a few hours."

"Extend it how?"

"I hear there's a great course up by Ruidoso, at the Inn of the Mountain Gods. The fairways wind through the mountains and the tee boxes are at some of the highest elevation in the country. You hit a golf ball at seven thousand feet," he offered as added inducement, "and it'll fly almost to the next county."

"You take a swing at seven thousand feet," Kate retorted, "and it's all you can do to suck in enough air for another."

Rueful laughter filled his eyes. "I've been sucking in a whole *bunch* of air this week. I can manage more than one swing if you can."

It was the laughter that snagged her, not the challenge. Kate had had a front-row seat this past week. She'd witnessed Dave's frustration, watched him push himself twice as hard as the team had pushed him. The fact that he could laugh at his failures— and had yet to brag about his successes—went a long way to altering her initial perception of him as just another hotshot sky jock.

She glanced at the narrow road winding toward the distant mountains. "Isn't Ruidoso a good hundred miles from here?"

"More or less."

"It'll take us all day to drive up there and squeeze in eighteen holes. We'll be driving back through the mountains at night."

"Unless we decide to stay over."

"Stay over? I didn't bring so much as a toothbrush with me. I don't usually need one to play golf," she tacked on with a touch of sarcasm.

"Ever hear of drugstores?"

Kate started to enumerate all the reasons why spinning a simple round of golf into a weekend expedition wasn't a good idea. Number one on her list was the fact that their agreement to focus strictly on Pegasus applied while on-site. How they handled matters off-site had yet to be negotiated.

To her disgust, Kate found that also topped her list of reasons to head for Ruidoso. She wasn't stupid or into self-denial. This man turned her on. She thought she'd been inoculated against handsome charmers like Dave Scott. Obviously, the inoculation had worn off.

He'd shown what he was made of this week. Maybe she should see what he was like away from their work environment. Discover if there was more to the man than that sexy body and his awesome skills as an aviator.

"Why don't we play this by ear?" she suggested. "See how long it takes to get there. And how we feel after eighteen holes."

"Sounds like a plan to me. Let me call and make sure we can get on the course this afternoon."

A quick call to information on his cell phone produced the number for the Inn of the Mountain Gods. The gods must have been smiling, because Dave managed to snag a 1:20 tee time that someone had just canceled. With a satisfied smile, he pocketed his cell phone, hooked an elbow on the window frame and aimed his pickup north.

*   *   *

Kate fell instantly in love with Ruidoso.

A onetime hideout of Billy the Kid, the old mining town was nestled high in the Sierra Blanca Mountains and surrounded by the Lincoln National Forest. Ski resorts, casinos, a racetrack, art galleries, boutiques and the many nearby lakes gave evidence that Ruidoso offered year-round fun for all ages and tastes.

Kate could envision the town blanketed in fresh white powder. Imagine it in summer, swarming with tourists eager to escape the blistering heat at lower elevations. Almost see the profusion of wildflowers that must carpet the high meadows in spring.

But she was sure fall *had* to be the most perfect time to visit. Tall green pines and blue spruce spilled down the slopes surrounding the town, interspersed with stands of oak, maple and aspen that added breathtaking splashes of color. Kate's delighted gaze drank in flaming reds, shimmering golds, impossibly bright oranges.

"Oh, boy. I hope this golf course of yours has scenery like this!"

It did. Owned and operated by the Mescalero Apaches, the resort was located on their reservation some miles out of Ruidoso. Mountains blazing with color surrounded the brand-new hotel and casino. Shimmering lake waters lapped at pebbled shores and reflected both the resort and the mountain peaks. The golf course, Kate saw as Dave parked in the lot behind a clubhouse constructed of pine and soaring glass, wasn't for the faint of heart.

The first hole—the very first!—required a clean shot over a stretch of clear blue lake to a small island. The second shot had to carry over water again to a raised green. Low bridges constructed of pine linked the island to shore and allowed access by cart.

"Forget handicaps!" Kate exclaimed. "We'll be lucky if we don't lose all our balls on the first hole."

Grinning, Dave hefted his bag. "Oh, no! You're not going to wiggle out of giving me strokes. I'm not handing you any advantage this time, Commander."

With another look at that killer first hole, Kate headed for the pro shop. Dave propped his bag on the rack by the door and followed her inside. His clubs, Kate noted, were well used and the finest that money could buy. Evidently the man took his golf as seriously as he did his flying.

The pro fixed her up with a decent rental set and they just had time to grab a lunch of Indian tacos washed down with ice-cold beer. Then Kate dragged a visor down low on her forehead to block the glare off the lake and teed up. After a few practice swings with a four iron, she sent her ball sailing across the water. It landed smack in the center of the small green island.

Dave gave a low whistle. "Nice shot."

"Thanks."

She couldn't help sashaying a bit as she strolled to the back of the tee box to help track his ball in flight. Not that it needed tracking. The little white sphere soared in a high, sweet arc and plopped down not two feet from hers.

When he turned to her with a smug grin, Kate knew the battle was on.

The war raged for seventeen holes.

Grudgingly, Kate gave him the strokes he demanded to even their games. She also voiced strong doubts about the twelve he supposedly carried as a handicap. Dave ignored her grousing and whacked ball after ball through the thin mountain air.

Kate had to pull out all the stops to stay even on the front nine, and led by two strokes as they approached number seventeen. It was a par three, only about a hundred and twenty yards from tee to green. In between was a sheer drop of a thousand feet or more!

Of course, she shanked her ball and lost it in the dense undergrowth at the bottom of the gully. That cost her two strokes, putting them even for number eighteen. They both made the green in regulation and the game boiled down to the final putt.

Dave was closer to the pin, so Kate putted first. It took her two tries to sink her ball. Not bad, considering how far out she'd been, but she held her breath while Dave lined up his shot. If he made this putt, he'd win.

He stroked the ball gently. His putter made its distinctive little *ping*. The ball rolled right for the cup—and stopped an inch short. Shaking his head, he walked up and dropped it in. His eyes held a glint of pure devilry when he retrieved his ball.

"How do you like that? Another tie."

Kate eyed him suspiciously. "Did you short that putt on purpose?"

"What do you think?"

It was the same answer he'd given her the first time they raced, and she didn't like it any better this time than she had then.

"Get this straight, Scott. When I play, I play to win."

He tossed his ball a few times, catching it in his palm. "Could be we're just well matched."

Belatedly, she remembered her ex had given him an earful. "And it could be," she said carefully, fighting the memory of old hurts and recriminations, "you think I'll get all bent out of shape if I lose."

"Win or lose, Hargrave, you couldn't get bent out of shape if you tried."

"I'm serious about this. I don't like the idea you're toying with me."

His fist closed around the ball. He fingered the dimples for a few moments before answering. "I like to win as much as you do. What I don't like is when healthy competition turns mean.''

Kate stiffened. ''As I'm sure my former husband told you happened in our marriage.''

''He implied something of the sort,'' Dave admitted with a shrug, ''but I wasn't thinking of your marriage when I said that.''

''Whose were you thinking of, then?''

''My brother's.'' His forehead creasing, Dave frowned at the ball still clutched in his hand. ''My sister-in-law is on his case all the time. About money. About the kids. Who's doing a better job with both. Ryan takes it, but it's eating him alive.''

''Why doesn't he walk?''

His gaze lifted and locked with hers. ''He says he loves her.''

''Funny thing about love.'' Kate managed to swallow the lump that suddenly formed in her throat. ''Sometimes it just plain hurts.''

''Well, I can't say I'm an expert on the subject, but I'll tell you this. I wouldn't walk, either, if I loved a woman as much as Ryan loves Jaci.''

''What would you do?''

''Find some way to call it a draw, I suppose.''

''Like this round of golf?''

His grin slipped out, quick and slashing. ''Like this round of golf.''

Kate wasn't sure, but she thought her heart did a funny little flip-flop at that point. How the heck could the man look so damned sexy with his checks singed red from the sun and his hair matted down from the ball cap he'd tugged on halfway through the game? Dragging her gaze from the tawny gold, she forced herself to concentrate as Dave offered a suggestion.

"Why don't we officially declare this game a tie and duke it out with another round tomorrow? If we arrange an early tee time, we can still make it back to the base by evening."

She breathed in the cool, clean air. Swept a glance at the riot of colors spilling down the mountain slopes. Brought her gaze back to the man who, despite her best efforts to hold him off, had somehow breached her barriers.

"You're on."

Dave had figured she couldn't resist the challenge. Hiding a smile, he dropped his putter back in his bag and waited for her to settle in the golf cart beside him.

His conscience didn't so much as ping at him for dangling the bait of another match. Golf was the last thing on his mind at this point. That was occupied with schemes to finesse Lieutenant Commander Kate Hargrave into bed.

Tonight. Right after dinner. Or before, if he could manage it.

God, he wanted her! Their morning runs had been enough to tie him in knots. Kate Hargrave in stretchy tights could tie *any* man in knots. Yet working with her this past week had added an entirely different dimension to his craving.

Dave had dated his share of beautiful women. He'd also worked alongside a good number of smart, dedicated ones. But Kate's particular combination of gorgeous and intelligent and dedicated was fast pushing the memory of all other females right out of his head.

He was still trying to lay out his game plan for the rest of the evening when they entered the two-story lobby of the resort. The pride the Mescalero Apaches took in their heritage showed in the soaring pine beams, the massive circular stone fireplace and the artistry of the woven rugs and baskets decorating the walls.

If the woman at the front desk took note of the fact that neither Kate nor Dave carried any luggage, she was too well-trained to show it. Her black eyes warm, she greeted them courteously.

"Welcome to the Inn of the Mountain Gods. May I help you?"

Dave returned her friendly smile. "We don't have a reservation, but would like to stay tonight. Do you have any vacancies?"

"Yes, sir, we do." Her fingers flew over a keyboard. "I can offer you a choice of views. Rooms with lake views are a little higher priced than those that look toward the mountains, but you'll consider

the extra twenty dollars well worth the cost when you
see the sunset.''

''A lake view it is then.''

''Will that be one room or two?''

Dave turned to Kate. She chewed on her lower lip,
and he decided he wouldn't rush her. Not until after
supper. He turned back to the clerk, intending to inform her they'd need two rooms, when Kate pre-
empted him.

''One room, please.''

Just in time, Dave choked back his words.

''Yes, ma'am,'' the clerk replied, unaware the
earth had just rocked under his feet. ''Would you
prefer smoking or nonsmoking?''

''Nonsmoking.''

''Two queen beds or one king?''

Dave sent a swift, silent prayer to the mountain
gods.

They answered his prayer. Or rather, Kate did.
With a small, private smile, she said the magic words.

''One king.''

Short moments later, they headed for the elevator.
Dave's blood was already drumming in his veins, but
he had Kate wait for him at the elevators while he
made a quick detour to the gift shop. He returned
with a small paper sack bearing the inn's distinctive
logo. Grinning, he responded to her look of inquiry.

''You said you needed a toothbrush.''

He'd purchased one for himself, too. Along with a box of condoms. With luck, stamina and a little ingenuity, he and Kate would run through the entire dozen before they had to return to the site tomorrow.

Six

Dave put both his ingenuity and his stamina to the test the moment the door to their minisuite thudded shut. He got a brief glimpse through the floor-to-ceiling windows of the still, silver lake and the neon eagle soaring above the casino. Ignoring both, he tossed the paper sack on a chair and snagged Kate's wrist.

A single tug spun her around. One step and he had her backed against the wall. Her head came up. Surprise flitted across her face.

"I warned you," Dave reminded her gruffly. "After our last kiss. No 'nice' this time."

Laughter leaped into her green eyes. "That still stings, does it?"

"Like you wouldn't believe."

"Seems I recall another part of the conversation. Didn't I say I'd give the signal when I was ready for you to conduct another test?"

"You already gave the signal. Downstairs. When you opted for one king."

"You're right. I did. Okay, flyboy, you have my permission to rev up to full throttle."

He was already there, Kate discovered when she slid her hands up his chest to his shoulders. The hard, roped muscles under her palms thrilled her. The rock-solid wall of his body against hers sent an arrow of pure sensation straight to her belly.

And when his mouth covered hers, Kate knew instantly nice was the last thing she wanted. She craved this heat, needed this hunger. The raw sensuality of her emotions stripped away any need for pretense. Every bit as greedy as Dave, Kate locked her arms around his neck and arched her body into his.

She was lost in his kiss, feeling its punch in every corner of her body, when he dragged his head up. Red singed his cheekbones. His breath came fast and hard. She thought he was going to gentle his touch, slow things down, and had to swallow a groan.

She thought wrong. With a skill that had to have come from plenty of experience, he tugged her knit shirt over her head, popped the snap on her slacks and stripped her down to her bra and panties. To

Kate's intense satisfaction, though, he was the one who groaned.

"Oh, baby." A callused palm shaped her breast, cradling its weight and fullness. "You couldn't count the hours I've spent imagining this moment."

She pretended to give the matter serious thought. Not an easy task with his thumb creating a delicious friction as it grazed over her nylon-covered nipple.

"Let's see. You've been on-site all of six days. Spent at least ten hours a day in the simulator, another five to six poring over tech manuals. If we subtract two for eating and six for sleeping, that doesn't leave much time for— Oh!"

She broke off, gulping, as he bent and replaced his hand with his mouth. His breath came hot and damp through the thin fabric of her bra, his tongue felt raspy on her now-engorged nipple. Her gulp turned to a swift, indrawn hiss when his teeth took over from his tongue.

"That left," he growled between nibbles, "plenty of time. To imagine this. And this."

Keeping one arm wrapped tight around her waist, he planed his other hand down the curve of her belly. His palm was hot against her skin, his fingers sure and strong when they cupped her mound. Within moments, Kate was a puddle of want.

She wasn't the kind to take and not give, though. Somehow, she managed to find the strength to put a few inches between them and drag his shirt free of his jeans.

"My turn, cowboy."

Dave ducked his head, more than willing to let her take the reins. His entire body ached with wanting her and he wasn't sure he could stand straight for much longer, but the glide of Kate's hands and mouth and tongue over his skin was worth the agony.

When she unsnapped his jeans and slid her palm inside, though, he came too damned close to losing it to remain standing. Scooping her into his arms, he headed for the bedroom. The sand-colored walls, prints of Apaches mounted on tough little mustangs, and incredible vista of lake and mountains alive with color imprinted on a small corner of his mind. A *very* small corner! The rest was filled with Kate. Gorgeous, sensuous, Kissable Kate.

She stretched like a cat on the luxurious down comforter. Her smooth, sexy curves made Dave's throat go tight. While he peeled off the rest of his clothes, she wiggled out of her bra and panties. Her glance measured his length, smiling at first, then with a greedy hunger that fed Dave's own. Rock hard and aching, he joined her on the bed and gathered her under him. His knee had wedged between hers before he remembered the damned sack.

"Hell!" He rolled off the bed in one lithe movement. "I'll be right back. Don't move."

Yeah, right! Kate thought wryly. As if she could!

Her heart hammered so hard against her chest she could hardly breathe, and everything from her waist down felt hot and liquid. She had a moment, only a moment, to wonder if she was crazy for tumbling into bed with a man who'd told her straight out he wasn't interested in any long-term relationships, before Dave was back with a full box of condoms. Kate's doubts disappeared on a gurgle of laughter.

"You don't really think we're going to need all those, do you?"

"A guy can only hope."

Opening the box, he dumped the contents on the bedside table. She was still chuckling when he rejoined her in bed. She welcomed him into her arms eagerly, hungrily, and into her body with a gasp of sheer delight.

Kate wasn't prepared for the intensity of the fire he stoked within her. He used his teeth and tongue and hard, driving body with a skill that soon had her writhing. The sensations piled one on top of each other, tight, hot, swirling. They came so fast and hard, Kate groaned out a warning.

"Dave! I can't...hold on!"

"So don't."

He flexed his thighs. His muscles in his back and butt went tight under her frantic fingers. Gasping, Kate tried to contain the wild sensations.

"I don't...want it to end...yet."

He lifted his head. His blue eyes held a wicked

glint. "Oh, sweetheart, it's just beginning. I swore I'd pay you back for every jolt and sickening drop you put me through, remember? This is just payback number one."

He flexed again, the sensations exploded, and Kate lurched almost out of her skin.

After that first frenetic coupling and several more not quite as fast but just as furious, they came up for air long enough to order a late dinner from room service.

Dave hit the showers while waiting for the delivery. Kate took her turn next and made good use of the toothbrush he'd purchased for her. Luckily, she had a comb in her purse to drag through her tangled hair. Wrapped in one of the inn's luxurious terrycloth robes, she joined Dave at the table beside the tall windows for a feast of crusty bread, crisp salad and mountain trout crusted with piñon nuts. A million stars glittered in the black-velvet sky outside, but Kate's mind wasn't on the spectacular nightscape. It was focused completely on the man across the table.

"Tell me more about your family," she asked him between bites. "Do you have any sisters or brothers besides the one you told me about?"

"Nope. There's just Ryan and me. Our folks died some years ago. How about you?"

"Both parents and three grandparents alive and well, along with three brothers, one sister."

"Are they all as good at what they do as you are?"

"Better," she said with a smile, thinking of all the support and encouragement her large, gregarious family gave each other. "My grandmother breeds and shows champion collies. My sister Dawn won a bronze in the Pan-American Games as a marathon runner and now coordinates the Special Olympics for a five-state region. One of my brothers is a fireman, another is on the pro tennis circuit. Josh, the baby of the family, is still in college. On a golf scholarship, I might add. I haven't beat him since his junior-high days, the stinker."

"So that's where you get it."

"Get what?"

"That mile-wide competitive streak. It's in your genes."

"Yes, it is."

She hesitated, reluctant to admit even now how much her inbred competitive spirit had played in the demise of her marriage.

"I tried to change," she confessed after a moment. "John—my former husband—interpreted my ambition and desire to excel as some sort of challenge to his masculinity. But the more I tried to hold back and suppress my natural instincts, the more I began to resent him for *wanting* me to hold back. There were other factors involved, of course."

Like a nineteen year old blonde, Kate thought sardonically.

"But the bottom line was he just didn't like being beat," Dave finished for her.

"That's about it." Kate laid down her fork. "Neither do you, or so you say. Yet every contest we've had so far has ended in a tie. Was that by chance or design?"

"You want the truth?"

"I asked, didn't I?"

"When we raced that first morning, I held back a little. *Only* because I was worried about your ankle," he added when Kate bristled. "I just about bust a gut trying to catch up to you the second time we raced."

That made her feel a little better.

"What about the putt you missed today?"

His mouth curved. "You didn't hear the four-letter words bouncing around inside my head after that stroke."

She tapped her fork against her plate, wanting to believe him. After her experience with John, she *needed* to believe him. There was no way she could change her basic personality and it was becoming increasingly important Dave know that right up front.

She was pushing a last, slippery little piñon seed around her plate when it occurred to her Dave couldn't change his basic personality, either. With a suddenly sinking feeling, she remembered her conversation with the weather officer at Luke.

"What about that?" she asked him, waving her fork at the rumpled bed. "How much of what just happened here is a game to you? One with tactical and strategic moves?''

''Oh, babe! All of it.''

Grinning, he pushed out of his chair and came around the table. A tug on the knotted tie of her robe brought Kate to her feet.

''I started scheming ways to finesse you into bed three and a half seconds after I spotted that turquoise spandex coming at me out of the dawn.''

''Why am I not surprised?'' Kate drawled.

''You shouldn't be.'' Unrepentant, he dropped a kiss in the warm V between her neck and shoulder. ''You, Lieutenant Commander Hargrave, are eminently finessable.''

''Is that supposed to be a compliment?''

''Of the highest order,'' Dave assured her solemnly, his fingers busy with the knot at her waist. The ties gave, and he slid his hands inside the folds to stroke the long, smooth curve from ribs to hips.

''Now, about dessert...''

''Yes?''

''I was thinking of something hot and sweet.''

Very hot and very sweet, he thought, his gut tightening as he slid his hand to the fiery curls at the juncture of her thighs. Slowly, he went down on one knee.

Kate woke to dazzling sunlight and the sound of running water. She rolled onto her side and watched

Dave slide a plastic razor through the lather covering his cheeks with sure, clean strokes.

He must have taken another shower. The tawny gold of his hair was still damp and water drops glistened on his bare back above the waistband of his jeans. Kate swallowed a sigh as her glance lingered on his perfect symmetry. Broad, muscled shoulders. A nice lean waist. That tight butt.

No doubt about it. The man was beautiful.

He was also, she reminded herself, taking a new vehicle into the sky for the first time tomorrow. A shadow seemed to cloud the sun as she thought about the two Pegasus prototypes that had crashed and burned. The pilot had been killed in the first one. The crew had survived the second, but sustained severe burns.

Kate had lost friends and associates to the vicious weather they routinely flew into. In her line of business, the risks were as great as the rewards. Yet the thought of Dave battling a violent wind shear or an engine stuck in half-tilt position made her feel sick.

She managed a smile, though, when he caught her watching in the mirror. You didn't talk about the odds. You just lived with them. Toweling his face, he strolled into the bedroom.

"We slept right through our tee time this morning."

"Did we?"

Kate couldn't get excited about missing a rematch

on the links. She'd stretched every muscle and tendon in her body last night, and then some. In fact, she wasn't sure she had enough strength to make it to the bathroom.

"We did," he confirmed, hitching a hip onto the side of the bed. "We also missed breakfast and lunch."

"Lunch?" Struggling up, Kate pushed the hair from her eyes. "What time is it?"

"Almost one."

"One?" she echoed incredulously. "As in p.m.?"

"As in p.m."

"Good grief!"

"Not to worry. I called down and arranged a late check-out." He waggled his eyebrows in an exaggerated leer. "So what do you want to do until two?"

"Well…"

By the time they finally abandoned their room and grabbed a late lunch in the hotel's dining room, it was after three. Yet Dave didn't seem any more anxious to end their stolen hours of freedom than Kate.

She'd checked in with her roommates by cell phone. Twice. Jill had already pinpointed their location via the tracking devices embedded in the IDs issued to both Kate and Dave, so there wasn't any use trying to deny they'd spent the night together. Promising to fill her and Caroline in later, Kate confirmed Captain Westfall hadn't returned from D.C. yet and hung up.

With no briefings or meetings pulling at them, she and Dave decided to take the slow way back to the site. From Ruidoso they headed south toward Cloud-croft. En route, the road meandered through the high mountain ridges and produced spectacular color at every turn. To Kate's delight, it also produced a turn-off for Sunspot.

"Who or what is Sunspot?" Dave asked.

"It's the home of the National Solar Observatory. *The* premier research facility for solar phenomena in the country. I've been wanting to visit for years."

She took a quick look at her watch, another at the mile indicator on the signpost, and calculated they could squeeze in a quick visit.

"Think they're open this late on a Sunday afternoon?"

"Not to the general public, maybe. But I've done some work with the observatory's director. If I drop his name a few times, maybe they'll let us poke around."

The sixteen-mile drive up to the observatory took a half hour and climbed over four thousand feet. Considering they were already at five thousand, Kate felt as though they'd reached the top of the world when they arrived at the cluster of buildings that constituted Sunspot, New Mexico. There was no restaurant, no grocery store, no services of any kind, so she could only hope the pickup had enough gas in it to get them back down the winding twists and turns.

What Sunspot did have, though, was a searingly blue New Mexico sky known for its clarity and transparency. For this reason, the U.S. Air Force had asked Harvard University to design a geophysics center on the site back in 1948 to observe solar activity. They started with a six-inch telescope housed in a metal grain bin ordered from Sears Roebuck. The site had since developed into a complex that included two forty-centimeter coronagraphs, high-tech spectrographs to measure light wavelengths and the Richard B. Dunn Solar Telescope—an instrument that was thirty stories tall and weighed some two hundred and fifty tons.

Kate couldn't wait to see it. Being able to show Dave some of her world was an added excitement.

"Park there by the gate," she instructed. "Let's go name-drop."

As it turned out, the only name Kate had to drop was her own. The director wasn't available, but his deputy happened to be on-site and came personally to escort her. Fence-pole thin and tanned to leather by the high altitude and thin air, the scientist pumped her hand.

"Dr. Hargrave! I'm Stu Petrie. This is an unexpected pleasure. I read your paper on the effects of ionization on water droplets spun up into the atmosphere by hurricane-force winds. *Most* impressive."

"Thank you. This is Captain Dave Scott, United States Air Force."

The deputy greeted Dave with a polite nod, but it was clear his interest was in Kate. So was Dave's, for that matter.

"Are you here on business? I didn't see a request from NOAA to use the facilities, but maybe it hasn't reached my desk yet. Sometimes the paperwork takes weeks to process."

"No, this is strictly spur of the moment. Dave and I were driving down from Ruidoso and saw the sign for the observatory. I couldn't resist taking a quick peek."

"We can do better than a peek. Please, let me give you a guided tour."

Dave's travels had afforded him the opportunity to view a good number of the world's marvels, both ancient and modern. The Dunn Telescope certainly qualified as the latter. The telescope's upper portion was housed in a tall, white tower that rose some thirteen stories into the air. The lower portion lay underground. The entire instrument was suspended from the top of the tower by a mercury-float bearing. The bearing in turn hung by three bolts, each only a couple of inches in diameter. Thinking about those nine meager inches didn't make Dave feel exactly comfortable when he followed the two scientists out onto the observing platform.

"The telescope is set to look at the quiet side of

the sun right now," Petrie said apologetically as Kate peered through its viewer. Dave took a turn and saw a dull gray ball.

"We use a monochrome camera to record the video image," Petrie explained. "This one is being taken in hydrogen alpha light, at about sixty-five hundred angstroms."

"Right."

Thankfully, Kate drew the scientist's attention with a comment. "You must use an electronic CCD to record the color images captured by your spectrographs."

"We do. With the Echelle Spectrograph we can measure two or more wavelengths simultaneously, even if they're far apart on the spectrum. We can also conduct near-ultraviolet and near-infrared observations."

Like most pilots, Dave had studied enough astrophysics to follow the conversation for the first few minutes. He knew near-ultraviolet and near-infrared light were just outside the visible range. After that, the two scientists left him in a cloud of dust.

He trailed along behind them, as fascinated by Kate's excitement and animated gestures as by her seemingly inexhaustible knowledge. She wasn't wearing a trace of makeup. She'd caught her hair back with a rubber band she'd snagged from the reservations clerk on the way out. Her knit shirt showed more than a few wrinkles from lying where Dave had tossed it the night before. She looked nothing like the spit-and-polish officer he'd worked with at the site. Even less like the runner in tight spandex.

Strange. Dave wouldn't have imagined she could replace either image in his mind, but her lively questions and the impatient way she tucked a loose strand behind her ear gave him a kick to the gut. Not as big a kick as Kate all naked and flushed from his lovemaking, of course. But close.

Busy studying her profile, Dave missed the comment that drew her auburn eyebrows into a quick, slashing frown.

"How much activity?" she asked Petrie.

They were talking about sunspots, Dave realized after a moment. The real thing, not the town. Evidently the folks at the observatory had recorded a buildup of energy in the sun's magnetic fields.

"There's definitely potential for eruptive phenomena."

That sounded serious enough for Dave to display his ignorance. "What's going to erupt where?"

Stu Petrie gave him the high school version. "Sunspots occur when the magnetic fields on the sun start to twist and turn. This movement generates tremendous energy, which is often released in a sudden solar flare."

"How much energy are we talking about?"

"Roughly the equivalent of a million hundred-megaton hydrogen bombs all exploding at once. The radiation is emitted across virtually the entire electro-magnetic spectrum, from radio waves at the long-wavelength end to optical omissions to X ray and gamma rays at the short-wavelength end. Given their tremendous speed, these waves can reach the earth in as little as eight minutes after a major flare and produce some very spectacular results.''

''Like the lights of the aurora borealis,'' Dave finished, feeling somewhat redeemed. Maybe he hadn't forgotten everything he'd learned about astrophysics after all.

''Solar flares can cause more than just lights in the sky,'' Kate put in, giving him a severe reality check. ''They can knock out power and fry electronics. In 1985, a flare blacked out Quebec. Another flare in 1998 knocked out the Galaxy 4 satellite and interrupted telephone pager service to some forty-five million customers.''

That caught Dave's attention. He was only hours away from going up in an aircraft crammed with the most sophisticated electronic circuitry yet devised. He wasn't real anxious for it to get fried while he was in the air.

''So, Doc,'' he asked Stu. ''What's the prognosis on this activity you're talking about?''

''We don't feel there's any cause for alarm at this point, but we're watching the energy buildup. Closely.''

''So will I,'' Kate muttered under her breath.

* * *

She left the National Solar Observatory considerably less relaxed than when she'd arrived. Her day didn't totally turn to crap, however, until Dave stopped to gas up in Chorro.

Seven

"Be right back," Kate said as Dave inserted his credit card into a gas pump. "I need to hit the ladies' room."

Busy squinting at the buttons in the dim glow cast by the moth speckled overhead light, Dave nodded. Dusk had fallen while they were still on the narrow winding road down from the observatory, followed by one of New Mexico's clear, star-studded nights.

A glimpse of the gas station's single, dingy rest room had Kate opting for the restaurant across the street. As she pushed through the doors of the Cactus Café, Bar and Superette, she was still mulling over her conversation with Stu Petric. Solar flares were a common enough occurrence. Nothing to become unduly alarmed about unless they gathered intensity and erupted with enough force to send huge pulses of energy hurtling through space. Then it was anyone's guess how much, if any, havoc the flares could wreak.

She'd stay in close contact with the National Solar Observatory over the next few days, Kate decided as she wove a path through the tables. Check their Web site regularly, just to see what was happening with those flares. That way she could…

"Hey!"

Jerked out of her thoughts, Kate turned to face a woman in tight black jeans, a puckered chambray top that left most of her midriff bare and dangling silver earrings. She held a plastic pitcher of iced tea in one fist. The other was planted on her hip.

"Did you just climb out of the pickup across the street?" the waitress asked Kate.

"Yes, I did. Why?"

The woman's glance flicked to Kate's left hand, noted the lack of rings, then shifted to the café's front window. It gave a clear view of the man at the pumps.

"I, uh, know the driver."

"Do you?"

"He stopped by the café a week or so ago. We hit it off, if you know what I mean."

Kate felt her limbs stiffen one by one. "I'm getting the picture."

"He had to leave early the next morning, said he was late for some business meeting. He promised he'd call me. Never did, though." She shook her head, smiling despite her obvious disappointment that Dave hadn't followed through. "That was some night, I can tell you."

"Yes, I'm sure it was."

The waitress—Alma according to her name tag—heaved a long sigh. "Oh, well, maybe you'll have more luck with him than I did. The handsome ones are always the hardest to bring to heel."

"That's what I hear. Where's the ladies' room?"

"Back of the café and to your left."

"Thanks."

Kate kept a tight smile on her face until she gained the privacy of the one-stall rest room. Slamming the bolt, she propped both hands on the chipped porcelain sink and let the idiot in the mirror have it.

"You dope! You almost fell for the guy. Him and his macho, do-it-till-we-get-it-right attitude in the simulator. And those morning runs! You let him invade your space, your solitude and your head."

The eyes staring back at her from the mirror blazed with scorn.

"You are *so* pathetic, Hargrave. He told you right up front he wasn't interested in long-term commitments. Hell, last night he admitted that he'd been scheming to get you into bed since day one, that it's all a game to him.''

He couldn't have laid things out any plainer! Yet just this morning Kate had gotten all warm and gooey inside and started thinking maybe, just maybe, she might have something going here.

''For a supposedly intelligent woman,'' she said in total disgust, ''you sure don't display many smarts when it comes to men.''

Furious with herself, Kate twisted the cold tap to full blast and splashed her face. The shock of the icy water and a thorough drying with rough paper towels went a long way to restoring her equilibrium. Forcing herself to get a grip, she leaned on the sink once more and lectured the face in the mirror.

''What the heck are you so mad about, anyway? You got off-site for a couple days. Shot a great round of golf. Indulged in some world-class sex. No promises of undying devotion were given or received, so there's no harm, no foul. On either side,'' she said sternly. ''Now it's back to business. Strictly business. Got that?''

Okay! All right! She got it.

She jerked the bolt and started to march out, but remembered her original purpose for exiting the pickup. Locking the door again, she hit the stall.

Alma was behind the counter in the café when Kate sailed through. The waitress popped her gum and flashed a rueful grin.

"Good luck, honey."

Kate didn't need luck. She had her head back on straight. But she returned the smile.

"Thanks. How about two cups of coffee to go?"

"You got 'em."

Dave was just finishing at the pump when she stepped outside.

"I brought you some coffee," Kate said, proud of her nonchalance

"Thanks." He took the cup she offered and downed a cautious sip. "Sure you don't want to grab something to eat?"

And have Alma wait on them? Hardly!

"We'd better get back to the site. Last time I talked to Jill, they had an ETA of twenty-one-hundred for Captain Westfall. If we push it, we can beat him back."

Taking care not to splash the hot coffee, Kate reclaimed her seat. Dave did the same.

"Jill didn't indicate the old man wanted to brief us tonight, did she?"

"No."

"Then what's the hurry? We've still got our toothbrushes and a few emergency supplies."

The crooked grin didn't work this time. If anything, it grated on Kate's nerves like fingernails scraping down a blackboard.

"There's a motel down the road a bit," Dave added while she fought to hang on to her temper.

"Nothing special like the Inn of the Mountain Gods, but clean and handy."

She just bet it was. No doubt Dave and Alma had made good use of it. Somehow, Kate managed to infuse her voice with just the right touch of amusement.

"Look, cowboy. This was fun, but playtime is over. It's time to get back to work."

"Fun?"

"Hey," she tossed off with a shrug, "fun is a big step up from nice. Let's go, Scott. It's getting late, I'm tired, and we both need to log in a good night's sleep before the flight tomorrow."

His eyes narrowed, but Kate was past caring. Her nonchalance meter had pegged out. Thankfully, he dropped the sexy, bantering tone and shoved the key in the ignition.

"Yes, *ma'am.*"

She wasn't up for any more talk. Reaching out, she flicked the switch on the CD player.

They passed through the last checkpoint a little before 9:00 p.m. Kate shoved her ID back in her pocket and waited impatiently until Dave pulled up outside her quarters. The squat, square modular unit had never looked so good. She reached for the handle and was out of the pickup before Dave had killed the engine.

"I'll see you tomorrow," she said. "Thanks for…for everything."

That was lame. Really lame. But the best she could do at the moment.

Evidently Dave shared the same opinion. His door slammed shut a half second after hers. Stalking around the front of the truck, he intercepted her straight path to her quarters.

"What the hell's going on here?"

She had her answer ready. She'd been working on it all the way in from Chorro.

"Nothing's going on here. Nothing *will* go on here. We're back on-site. We declared this a no-fly zone, remember?"

"Sure felt like we made some changes to the rules last night."

"Last night we were off base," Kate said stubbornly. "We'd been ordered to relax, relieve some stress. We're back now and—"

"Relieve some stress!" he interrupted, his eyebrows snapping into a scowl. "Is that what you thought we were doing?"

His apparent anger surprised her. She would have guessed Dave Scott would be the first to argue that sex was the perfect antidote for everything. She couldn't resist getting a little of her own back.

"Come on, Scott. You have to admit you're a whole lot looser than when you left yesterday."

"I was," he retorted. "That looseness seems to have dissipated in the last half hour or so."

Feeling considerably better than when she'd walked out of the Cactus Café, Kate smiled. "Sounds like you've got a problem, cowboy. See you tomorrow."

Dave had a problem, all right. It was sashaying away from him at the moment. Folding his arms, he propped his hips against the fender of his pickup and tried to figure out what the heck just happened.

Kate couldn't be serious about this "not-on-site" stuff. Not after last night. Not to mention this morning. The mere memory of her smooth, slick skin and smoky taste had his throat going tight.

He was as serious about the mission as the next guy. More so. He was the one who'd put his life on the line when Pegasus lifted off, for Pete's sake. So where did Kate get off suggesting he was such a jerk he couldn't concentrate on her *and* on the mission at the same time?

And why did he want to?

That last thought brought him up short. Frowning, he stared at the door Kate had just disappeared through. Okay, they'd had some great sex. Better than great. He got a hitch in his breath just thinking about it. But the lady had made her druthers clear and Dave didn't usually push so hard or so long after being waved off.

Still frowning, he shoved away from the fender and headed for his own quarters.

"Please tell me it was awful," Cari begged as Kate dropped onto the sofa. "I've already wormed a report out of Jill and I'm not sure I can take being the only sex-starved female officer on-site. Tell me Scott's only so-so in bed."

"Scott is excellent in bed. He's also a total jerk. No, that's not right. I'm the jerk."

Obviously that wasn't the answer Cari expected. Blinking, the Coast Guard officer laid aside her dog-eared paperback. "What happened?"

Kate blew out a long breath. "We drove up to Ruidoso, played some golf, hit the sack."

"And the problem with that sequence of events is…?"

"There wasn't any problem," Kate admitted wryly, "until we stopped for gas on the way back and I bumped into Dave's little bit of 'personal business.' The one who caused him to call in and delay his arrival on-site," she added at Cari's puzzled look.

"Uh-oh."

"Right. Uh-oh."

The brunette bit her lip. She knew Kate had good reason to be wary of too-handsome, love-'em-and-leave-'em types like Dave Scott. Still, anyone standing within fifty yards of the weather officer and the sky jock had felt the heat from the sparks they'd been striking off each other since the first day Scott appeared on the scene.

"In all fairness," she pointed out, "Dave obviously met that little bit of personal business, as you term her, before he met you."

"True."

"And he hasn't been off-site since he got here—except with you."

"Also true."

"So why do you think you're a jerk for having a nice steamy weekend fling with the guy?"

When her roommate didn't answer right away, Cari's eyes widened. "We *are* talking just a weekend fling, aren't we?"

"Of course we are. I guess."

"Kate!"

"I know, I know! It's just... Well, for a crazy moment or two I was starting to think it might be something more. Stupid, huh?"

"Not necessarily," Cari countered, recovering from her surprise.

"Yes, it was. *Very* stupid. We'll only be here for another month at most, after which we'll all return to our respective units."

"So you go back to MacDill and Dave returns to Hurlburt. The two bases are both in the Florida panhandle, not more than a hundred or so miles apart."

"A hundred miles is a hundred miles," Kate said doggedly. "I learned the hard way that long-distance relationships don't work. Not for me, anyway. Besides which," she added with a shrug, "Dave made it clear his first or second day on-site he's not in the market for anything long term."

"He did?"

"He did."

Kate's ready sense of humor inched its way through the funk that had gripped her since her encounter with Alma.

"We got in one heck of a round of golf, though. I have to admit the man has a great swing."

"I'll bet."

"Oh, and we stopped at the National Solar Observatory on the way back."

"Golf, sex *and* the National Solar Observatory." Cari rolled her eyes. "What more could a girl ask for?"

Her amusement disappeared when Kate related the news about possible solar-flare activity. Having spent most of her career on the water, the Coast Guard officer had learned to pay serious attention to any unusual weather activity.

They were still discussing the potential impact on the Pegasus test program when Jill returned from one of the perimeter checks she ran at random times.

"Hey, you finally made it back," she said to Kate. "How was your, uh, golf game?"

"Terrific. How was yours?"

"Terrific," Jill replied, laughing. Tossing aside her

fatigue cap, she raked her fingers through her blunt-cut collar-length hair. "So? What's the scoop? Is Dave Scott as good with his hands out of the simulator as he is in it?"

"Better. As I was just telling Cari."

Kate lifted her arms in a lazy stretch. She was fine now, over her brief spate of lunacy. She'd let down her guard for a few hours and Alma had jerked it back up. She owed the woman for that.

"And as I told Dave a few minutes ago," she continued, "the weekend was fun. But now it's over and we both need to concentrate on more important matters."

Jill's eyebrows soared. "Fun? You told him it was fun? How did our hotshot pilot take that?"

Not as well as Kate had expected, surprisingly. She supposed she could have phrased things a little more politely, but she'd been in no mood to stroke the man's ego at that point.

"He took it," she said dismissively, and deliberately changed the subject. "Did Captain Westfall get back?"

"He's twenty minutes out," Jill confirmed. "Rattlesnake Control just notified me. They also relayed a message from the boss. He wants the senior test-cadre personnel to convene at his quarters as soon as he touches down."

"Any idea why?"

"Not a clue. I've already notified Russ McIver.

He'll pass the word to Dave. Consider this your official notification."

Kate surged off the couch. "I better scrub away some of this road dust and get into my uniform."

Cari was right behind her. They took turns in the tiny, closet-size bathroom and bumped elbows squeezing past each other in the narrow hall. Brushed, buffed and uniformed, they were ready when Rattlesnake Control confirmed the captain had returned to the site.

The three women walked the short distance to the captain's quarters. Dave and Russ were already there, along with the senior civilian test engineers. Kate gave the men a friendly smile, Dave included. He returned it, but a crease formed between his eyebrows and stayed there until Captain Westfall called the impromptu meeting to order.

"The good news is that the Joint Chiefs are pleased with the way we've gotten the Pegasus test schedule back on track. I told General Bates that was due in large part to your skill, Captain Scott."

Dave took the news that Captain Westfall and the air force's top-ranking four-star general had discussed his abilities with a nod.

"General Bates suggested our progress probably had more to do with your tenacity than your expertise," Westfall added, his gray eyes glinting. "He

had a few words to say about your insistence on doing a task again and again until it gets done right."

"I was in the left seat when he took the Osprey
up for the first time," Dave explained with a grin.
"I failed him—on that check ride and the next."

"So he indicated."

Sobering, Westfall glanced around the group.
They'd formed a tight bond, officers and civilians
alike. Some tighter than others, he suspected. Normally he wouldn't tolerate fraternization within the
ranks, but this small test cadre represented a unique
set of circumstances. Although the six uniformed officers had chopped to him for the duration of the
Pegasus project, they still reported to their respective
services. More to the point, they were all experts in
their fields. Each of them was vital to a project that
had just jumped the tracks from fast to urgent.

"The bad news is that all hell is about to break
loose in Caribe."

"Again?" Russ McIver shook his head. "The island has gone through three coups in two years, each
one bloodier than the last. I thought the U.S. had
poured enough money and troops into the area to
keep this president in office for more than a few
months."

"That's the problem. We poured in too many
troops, some of whom are now needed on the other
side of the globe. The Pentagon intends to withdraw
elements of the 101st and the 2nd Marine MAF. They

also want to speed up the air and sea trials of Pegasus. The thinking is that Pegasus would make a perfect insertion vehicle if it becomes necessary to go back into Caribe in a hurry.''

"No problem with the sea trials, sir," Caroline said firmly. "I'll take a look at the test schedule and see what runs we can shave off."

"Good. Captain Scott?"

"Pegasus is ready to fly, sir. So am I. We'll test our wings tomorrow."

Eight

Pegasus took to the sky like the mythical winged steed it was named for.

Two chase vehicles accompanied it. The first was the site's helo. Painted in desert colors, the chopper hovered like an anxious brown hen while Pegasus rose slowly from the desert floor. Russ McIver viewed the prototype's ascent from the chopper's cockpit.

"We've got you at fifty feet, Pegasus One. Seventy. One hundred."

"Confirming one hundred feet, Chase One."

His hands and feet working the controls, Dave held the hover. Sand blew up from the rotors' downwash and obliterated any view outside the cockpit windows, but he kept his gaze locked on the instruments and ignored the whirlwind.

Like the tilt-winged Osprey that was its predecessor, Pegasus was designed to lift off from small, unimproved patches of dirt, fly long and hard, and drop down in another small patch. Dave maintained the hover for a good ten minutes before taking the craft back down. Foot by foot, inch by inch, with the desert sand whirling in a mad vortex until the wide track tires just kissed the dirt.

After three more touch and go's, he was ready to switch to cruise mode. He brought the vehicle back up to a hundred feet, retracted the wheels into the belly of the craft, and ran through a mental checklist before sucking in a deep breath.

"Pegasus One, preparing to tilt rotors."

"Roger, One."

At ten degrees tilt, the test vehicle still handled like a helicopter. Dave nosed it forward, added speed and increased the tilt. The craft bucked a bit at thirty degrees, then the blades on the two engines began slicing air horizontally instead of vertically. Dave pushed the throttles forward and Pegasus took the bit. Within moments he had gained both altitude and airspeed.

Chase One kept up with them for the first few miles. Chase Two took over as the chopper fell behind.

"Pegasus One, this is Chase Two. We've got you in sight. You're lookin' good."

The C-130 Hercules and its crew were detached from the 46th Test Operations Group at Holloman AFB, New Mexico. The highly instrumented aircraft had been designed for just this purpose—observing and testing the latest in sophisticated weaponry. Kate and a team of evaluators were on board to serve as observers for the long-distance portion of the flight. Straining against her shoulder harness, she peered over the flight engineer's shoulder at the sleek white vehicle streaking through the sky. The Herc's pilot kept Pegasus just off his left wing.

"Look at that baby move," she heard him comment to his copilot. "He's approaching a hundred and fifty knots and still piling on the airspeed."

Kate's heart stayed firmly lodged in her throat as Dave pushed Pegasus to perform at maximum capacity. Both the test vehicle and its chase plane reached two hundred knots, with the desert sliding by below them in a blur of silver and tan. Two-twenty. Two-thirty.

"Control, this is Pegasus One."

Dave's voice came through Kate's headset, cool and calm above the background static.

"I'm feeling a vibration in the right aft stabilizer area."

Test Control came on immediately. "Are you showing any system malfunction or warning lights?"

"Negative, Control."

"Is the vibration such that it could affect the structural integrity of the tail section?"

Kate held her breath. That was a judgment call, pure and simple. An educated guess based on the pilot's expertise and familiarity with his craft. A sick feeling gripped her as she remembered that one of the first two prototypes had gone down after a structural stress fracture almost took off a wing. She could hardly hear Dave's reply through the pounding of her heart.

"Negative, Control. He's giving me a bumpy ride, but not trying to buck me off."

"Copy that, Pegasus One. We recommend you decrease your airspeed to two hundred knots. Let us know if the vibration continues."

"Roger."

Kate strained forward. Her harness straps cut into her shoulders. A vein throbbed in her left temple. She counted the seconds until Dave came on again.

"Airspeed now at two hundred knots and I'm not feeling the tail shudder."

The controller didn't try to disguise his relief. "Roger that, Pegasus One. Recommend you keep the airspeed below two hundred for the duration of this flight."

"Will do."

Gulping, Kate tore her gaze from the vehicle across a stretch of blue sky and checked the Doppler radar screen. It showed clear, no sign of weather within the projected flight pattern, but she used the satellite frequency assigned to her to call for regular updates throughout Pegasus's first flight.

It lasted for one hour and seventeen seconds. Dave took the craft in a wide circle over the New Mexico desert, testing the flight-control systems at various altitudes. By the time he slowed the vehicle, rotated the engines from horizontal to vertical and set down in the same patch of dirt he'd lifted off from, Kate was a puddle of sweat inside her flight suit.

The C–130 landed at an airstrip bulldozed out of the desert specifically for the Pegasus tests. The crew piled out as soon as the pilot shut down his craft, then boarded the waiting shuttle to take them back to Test Operations for the mission debrief. There they congratulated a sweaty, grinning Dave Scott.

"Good ride, Captain." The C–130's pilot pumped his hand. "You really put that baby through his paces."

The navigator, who had evidently flown with Dave before, pounded him on the back. "Sierra Hotel, Scott."

Kate hid a smile at the aviators' universal shorthand for shit hot, but her congratulations were every bit as sincere.

"You did good, Captain."

"Thanks, Commander." The tanned skin beside

his eyes crinkled. The glint in their blue depths was intended for her alone. "How about we get together later this evening and review the flight-test data?"

With the thrill of success still singing in her veins, Kate had to force herself to remember Alma. And Denise. And who knew how many other women this man had charmed with that same wicked glint. Keeping an easy smile on her face, she sidestepped the invitation.

"I have a feeling Captain Westfall will want to pore over every bit of data right here, right now."

She was right. They spent the next three hours reviewing every phase of the flight and analyzing instrument readings. Captain Westfall was particularly concerned about the vibration and asked the engineers to examine every inch of the tail section before the next flight, scheduled for the following Thursday.

That was only four days away. Barely enough time to make any changes or corrections in either the instrumentation or the body of the vehicle itself if necessary. Chewing on her lower lip, Kate gathered her stack of computer analyses and stuffed them in her three-ring binder for additional review tomorrow. From her experience during the land phase of testing, she knew the euphoria from the flight would have subsided by then and reality would set in with a vengeance.

Dave and Russ were the first to arrive at the picnic table later that evening. Jill Bradshaw soon joined them. She'd spent the day racing across the desert in a souped-up Humvee, directing ground security for the flight. If Pegasus had gone down, she and her troops would have had to secure the crash site immediately. She was still in uniform and her cheeks showed a flush of red sun and windburn below the white patches made by her goggles.

"You look like you could use a cool one," Russ commented, pulling a beer from the ice chest.

"I could. A *long* cool one." She took the dripping can, popped the top and clinked it against Dave's. "In all the hubbub this afternoon, I didn't get to offer my congrats. Good flight, Scott."

"Thanks."

Caroline Dunn joined the group a few moments later, followed in short order by Doc Richardson and Captain Westfall. Isolated by the responsibility of command, Westfall didn't often unbend enough to gather with his subordinates. Tonight marked a definite exception.

Gradually, the tension that had held Dave in its grip since early morning slid off his shoulders. Just as gradually, a different kind of tension took hold.

"Where's Kate?" he asked Cari during a lull in the conversation.

"At her computer. She said she wanted to review the latest reports from the solar observatory."

Dave nodded and tipped his beer, but it didn't go

down with quite the same gusto as it had before. Nor could he shake the urge to slip away from the crowd, rap on Kate's door, and sweet-talk her into a private little victory celebration. He could almost feel her curves and valleys against his body. Taste her on his tongue. He didn't realize his fist had tightened around the beer until the can crumpled and slopped cold liquid over his hand.

"Damn!"

Laughing, Cari passed him a paper napkin. "Good thing your hand was steadier this morning."

He gave the Coast Guard officer a sheepish grin and was about to reply, when her cell phone buzzed. Everyone on-site had been issued special instruments that picked up the signals from their personal phones and relayed them through a series of secure networks to the test site. Friends and relatives could still keep in touch, but no one would find any record of calls made to or from this particular corner of New Mexico.

Flipping open the phone, Cari put it to her ear. "Lieutenant Dunn. Oh, hi, Jerry."

She listened a moment and a smile come into her eyes. "No kidding? I bet that was something to see."

Holding her hand over the mouthpiece, she excused herself from the group and walked a little way away.

"Jerry again," Jill muttered to Cody. "I wish the man would get a life."

Cody nodded. Russ McIver frowned into his beer. Obviously the only one in the dark, Dave voiced a question.

"Who's Jerry?"

"A navy JAG," Jill answered. "He calls Cari every few days."

Dave lifted an eyebrow. "Sounds serious."

"He'd like it to be."

"But?"

Jill hesitated, obviously reluctant to discuss her friend's personal life. Once again, Dave sensed he was still an outsider, that the rest of the group had yet to fully accept him into their tight little circle. It was left to Doc Richardson to fill in the gaps.

"Commander Wharton has three kids by an ex-wife. Evidently he has some reservations about starting another family while he's still on active duty."

Dave could understand that. He'd seen how tough it was for air force couples to juggle assignments and child care. Throwing long sea tours into the equation would make it even tougher.

Russ McIver voiced the same reservations. "The guy has a point. Be hard to raise kids with one parent at sea and the other deployed to a forward area."

"I've seen it done," Captain Westfall said calmly. "It takes a lot of compromise and a couple as devoted as they are determined."

Mac was too well trained to contradict his superior,

but his disagreement showed on his face as he eyed
the small, neat figure some yards away.

The gathering broke up soon after that. Still too
hyped from his flight, Dave wasn't ready to hit the
sack. The urge to rap on Kate's door and coax her
out into the night was still with him. He managed to
contain it with the knowledge he'd have her to himself tomorrow morning when they went for their run.

She didn't show.

Dave waited in the chilly dawn while reds and
golds and pinks pinwheeled across the sky. Arms
folded, hips propped against the fender of his pickup,
he watched the glorious colors fade in the slowly
brightening sun. They seemed to burn brighter and
take longer to dissipate, just as the minutes seemed
to drag by. Finally he shoved back the sleeve of his
sweatshirt and checked his watch. If he pushed it,
he'd have time to get in a quick five miles before
breakfast and the round of postflight briefings scheduled for 0800.

He worked up a solid sweat and a fierce hunger
on the punishing run. A dark V patch arrowed down
the front of his shirt. His drawstring sweatpants felt
damp at the small of his back. Swiping his forearm
over his face, Dave made for the dining hall. He'd
scarf up some of the cook's spicy Mexican scramble,
hit the showers and track Kate down before the meeting to find out why she'd missed her run.

He didn't have to track far. She came out of the dining hall just as Dave was going in. He stopped, frowning as he took in the towel draped around the neck of her warm-up suit and the perspiration glistening on her cheeks and temples.

"What's going on? Did you change your exercise routine?"

"It's getting a little too cool in the mornings for me. I decided to use the treadmill in the gym instead."

"You could have told me about the change in plans. I waited a half hour for you."

"Sorry."

She looked anything but. Dave's jaw tightened. He had received his share of brush-offs, but none of them had left him both angry and frustrated. Kate was doing a helluva job at both.

"We need to talk about the other night," he told her brusquely.

"No, we don't."

"C'mon, Kate. I'm not buying this on-site, hands-off crap. What's the problem here?"

She opened her mouth, shut it, then tried again.

"The problem is me. I've discovered I can't combine fun and work without one slopping over into the other. So one has to give."

"When did you make this big discovery?"

"After talking to Alma."

"Who?"

She stared at him for long moments. "Never mind. She's not important. What's important is Pegasus. That's why we're here, Dave. And that's why the on-site, hands-off rule will stay in effect."

She issued the edict as if expecting him to snap to, whip up a salute and bark "Yes, *ma'am!*"

Dave wasn't about to bark anything. Cocking his head, he weighed his options and chose the one he suspected she would least expect.

"You don't have to cut out your morning run. I'll take mine in the evenings. In exchange, you stop treating me as though I'm some plebe at the academy who needs to be reminded of his purpose in life every hour on the hour."

Her startled expression had him shaking his head.

"It's called compromise, Hargrave. I give a little. You give a little. Before you know it, we've found a satisfactory solution to this problem we appear to have."

He left her at the door, feeling pretty smug. It was good to see *her* knocked off balance for a change. She'd sure as heck kept Dave flying a broken pattern almost from the day he'd arrived.

He didn't realize how broken until two nights later.

The compromise he'd proposed wasn't working. Not for him, anyway. He missed his early-morning runs with Kate and her collection of spandex. He even missed her officious tone when she'd tried to pull rank or put him in his place. All he got from the woman now were cool smiles and polite nods that left him edgy and frustrated and hungering for the fire he knew smoldered inside her.

It took a call from his brother to open his eyes to the truth. Like Caroline's JAG, Ryan was patched through a series of relay stations that gave him no clue where Dave was. Not that Ryan particularly cared. He was too used to his brother's nomadic lifestyle—and on this particular occasion too drunk—to question his whereabouts.

"Hey, bro," he got out, the slur thick and heavy. "I thought I'd better call you and give you the news."

Dave propped himself up on an elbow and squinted at the bedside clock: 2:30 a.m. New Mexico time. Four-thirty back in Pennsylvania. Alarm skittered along his nerves. Ryan drunk was a rare occurrence. Ryan drunk and out all night had never happened before. Not to Dave's knowledge.

"What news, Ry?"

"Jaci and me. We're calling it quits."

"Aw, hell!"

"That's what I said. Right before I walked out."

Ryan burped, thunked the phone against something and cursed.

"I couldn't take it anymore," he said a moment later. "I tried. The Lord knows, I tried."

"Yeah, you did. Where are you now?"

"I'm at my office."

It figured. Over the years Ryan's office had become more than a workplace or source of income. It had become his refuge, his retreat when the arguments got too heated and too hurtful. Struggling upright, Dave punched the pillow behind him and tried not to wince when a pitying whine crept into his brother's voice.

"I still love her. That's the rotten part. I can't imagine life without Jaci and the kids."

"So don't imagine it."

"Huh?"

"You're drunk, Ry. You need to sleep this off, then go home and talk to your wife. See if you can't work a compromise."

"What kind of compromise?"

"Hell, I don't know. Maybe if you spend a little less time at the office and a little more with Jaci and the kids, she'll get off your back some."

"Thass what she says."

Another morose silence descended, interspersed with some heavy breathing.

"Dave?"

"I'm here."

"I'm drunk. I'm going to sleep it off."

"Good idea."

"Dave?"

"What?"

"Have you ever wanted a woman so bad you ached with it?"

All the time, bro.

His brain formed the flip reply, but the words stuck in his throat. The truth came out of the darkness and hit him smack in the gut.

"As a matter of fact, Ry, I'm kind of in that situation now."

He waited for a response. All that came over the phone was a loud snore.

"Ry! Hey, Ryan!"

"Huh?"

"Hang up the phone, man. Then get some sleep and talk with Jaci in the morning."

"Yeah."

The receiver banged down. Wincing, Dave flipped his cell phone shut and dropped it on the bedside table. He took a long time going back to sleep. Worry for his brother was a habit that went deep. Ryan and Jaci had been going at each other for a long time. Dave only hoped they'd find a way to patch things up.

In the meantime, he had another problem to keep him awake. One that came packaged with flaming copper hair, a mouth made for kissing and a bone-deep stubborn streak.

Here, alone in the dark, Dave could admit the truth. He ached for Kate. Physically *and* mentally. The feeling was as unsettling as it was unfamiliar.

Hooking his hands behind his head, he stared up at the ceiling and tried to figure out when lust had slipped over into something deeper, something he wasn't quite ready to put a name to yet.

He couldn't pinpoint the exact moment, but to his surprise he suspected it had happened well before their weekend in Ruidoso. He'd wanted Kate in his bed, sure. He *still* wanted her in his bed. Looking back, though, he realized he'd come to crave her laughter and her company as much as her seriously gorgeous body.

The realization had him scowling up into the darkness. Okay, he wanted Kate. All of her. Like he'd never wanted another woman. The problem now was what the hell to do about it.

Nine

Dave made his move the next evening.

The timing was iffy. The entire test cadre had been going full out for three days to analyze the data from the first flight and prepare for the second. The engineers hadn't been able to pinpoint what caused the vibration in the tail section. With the second flight scheduled for tomorrow afternoon, Dave had insisted on more hours in the simulator to practice emergency responses to possible structural failures. By the time he climbed out around six that evening, he felt as though he'd been ridden hard and put away wet.

A long shower and a hearty meal of steak and home fries revived him. So did the prospect of getting

Kate alone for an hour. He caught her on her way back to Test Operations. Unlike Dave, she was still in uniform. The sky blue of her zippered flight suit formed a perfect foil for the fire of her hair.

"I thought we were done for the day," he commented, falling in beside her.

"I thought so, too. But tomorrow's flight is going to take you into the mountains and I want to review the wind patterns one more time. I wouldn't want you to run into another katabatic wind," she added, her lips curving.

It was the first real smile Dave had received from her in days. He felt like a kid who'd just been handed a fistful of penny candy.

"Trust me, I have no desire to get hit with another whammy like that one. Think it's possible?"

"Highly unlikely. The air temperatures at the higher altitudes are dropping significantly, but there's no snow on the peaks yet. You could experience some severe downdrafts, though."

"I'm wondering if that's all I'll experience. Did you notice a greenish glow in the sky when you were running this morning?"

She threw him a sharp look. "No."

"I saw it last night while I was running along the perimeter road. It was hanging low in the northern sky. I just caught a glimpse of it through the peaks."

"What time was that?"

"About eight-forty."

Her eyebrows drew into a frown. "I didn't see any reports of unusual light patterns on the weather sites this morning."

"The glow only lasted for a short while, maybe two or three minutes."

Dave wasn't lying. Not exactly. He *had* noticed a dim glow, but it was more smoky than green. Anything could have caused it. A dust cloud thrown up by a passing vehicle. A low-hanging storm cloud scudding across the sky, lit from within by the moon. Given the recent reports of possible solar-flare activity, though, he'd figured Kate would want to check it out.

Sure enough, she took the bait. Still frowning, she checked her watch. "It's eight-fifteen now. Can you show me where you spotted this glow?"

"I'll get my truck and drive you out there. We should just make it."

The pickup jounced along the unmarked dirt track that served as the site's perimeter road. Dave checked the odometer, squinted at the dark shapes to the north and pulled over.

"This is about where I spotted the lights." Leaning across Kate, he pointed to the jagged ridgeline. "Over there, through those peaks."

She reached for the door handle, but Dave stilled her with a quick warning. "We'd better notify Security before we climb out. We're right on the perimeter. Their sensors are probably already flashing red alert.''

All it took was a quick press of one key on his specially configured cell phone to connect him with Security Control.

''This is Captain Scott. I'm out along the perimeter road, 3.2 miles into the northwest quadrant.''

''We've got you on the screen, Captain Scott.''

''Commander Hargrave is with me. We're going to step out of our vehicle.''

''We'll track you. Watch where you walk. You don't want to put your boot down in a nest of diamondbacks.''

Dave didn't take the warning lightly. He'd heard that one of Jill Bradshaw's cops had done exactly that before he'd arrived on-site.

Kate was doubly cautious. ''I listened in via the radio net with the rest of the test cadre that night when Jill and Doc Richardson jumped a chopper and raced to the injured cop. That wasn't an experience I'd want to see repeated. We'd better not stray too far from the truck.''

That suited Dave just fine.

''No problem. I'll just back it around and let down the tailgate. We can perch there while we wait for the show.''

With the truck in position, he and Kate climbed out. They couldn't have asked for a better night for star watching. Above the black mass of the mountains, the sky was deep and dark. A couple of million stars shone with the brilliance only visible at these high altitudes. The nip in the night air had Dave reaching into the back seat for a worn leather bomber jacket. When he offered it to Kate, she declined.

"You'd better put it on. My flight suit will keep me warm."

When Dave lowered the tailgate, Kate propped her hips on the edge. He opted to stand and watch the northern sky for signs of unusual activity. The moments slid by with only the still, dark night around them. Kate checked her watch a couple of times. Dave couldn't tell from her expression whether she was relieved or disappointed that nothing happened.

"I got a call from my brother last night," he said after a while.

She angled her head around. "The one having problems with his marriage?"

"That's the one. Ryan said he and Jaci are calling it quits."

"Ouch." Her face softened in sympathy. "Been there, done that. It's not fun."

"Didn't sound like it from Ryan's perspective."

"What made him finally decide to walk?"

"I'm not sure. He was pretty drunk when he called. I couldn't get much out of him."

"You said they love each other despite their problems. Maybe they'll patch it up."

"Maybe." He hadn't forgotten her remark that

love can sometimes hurt. "What about you? What made you decide to walk?"

Her mouth twisted into a rueful grimace. "A nineteen-year-old blonde. Evidently she was just what my ex needed to stroke his ego after the way I'd pounded it into the dust. His phrasing, not mine, by the way."

"In other words, he couldn't keep up with you on the golf course."

"Or off it." Her shoulders lifted under the blue Nomex of her flight suit. "Took me a while to stop feeling guilty about that."

"Is that why you skittered away from me after we got back from Ruidoso? You were afraid I couldn't keep up with you on or off the course?"

"I didn't skitter away. I merely redrew the lines we had already established."

"The lines *you* had established. I've been thinking about those."

He pushed away from the fender. A single step placed him in front of her. His hands slid up her arms, gliding over the smooth fabric of her flight suit. With a gentle tug, he pulled her to her feet.

"Dave, we agreed. Not on-site."

"Well, technically we're off-site. I angled the truck around. The tail end is sticking clear over the perimeter road."

Anger flared hot and quick in her eyes. Planting her palms flat on his chest, she stiff-armed him. "So this was all a ploy? A ruse to get me out here?"

"Partly. I did see a strange glow last night. I also wanted to get you back on neutral ground, so we can rekindle the fires we lit last weekend."

"We can't." Jerking free of his loose grip, she folded her arms. "And even if we could, I don't want to compete with Denise and Alma."

"Denise I remember," Dave said, exasperated, "but only because you keep bringing her into the conversation. Who the heck is Alma?"

"She's a waitress at the Cactus Café. About five-five. Brown hair. Lots of mascara. Remember her?"

"Now I do," he replied with a sheepish grin.

Talk about ironic. Dave had been sure he'd never forget that wild night. Since tangling with Kate, though, he could barely remember his name at times, let alone his carefree days before he arrived on-site.

"Let me guess," he said wryly. "You bumped into Alma when we stopped to gas up in Chorro."

"Bingo."

"And she's the reason you've been giving me the deep freeze all week?"

Arms still folded, she tapped a foot and considered her answer. Dave had spent enough time with her by now to know she wouldn't dodge the issue.

"Alma is part of the reason," Kate admitted at last. "Only because she made me face up to hard, cold reality. The problem is it's impossible to keep personal feelings from slopping over into our professional situation. For me, anyway. The thought of being the latest in your string of weekend flings made me furious until—''

''I'm not keeping score,'' Dave interrupted dryly. ''You can check my bedpost. You won't find any notches carved there.''

''Until I realized I had no right to be angry,'' she finished firmly. ''We had some fun, that's all. Neither one of us made any promises. I had no reason to feel hurt or jealous. More to the point, I don't *want* to feel hurt or jealous. Not again.''

''I can't change the past, Kate. Nor am I going to apologize for it. But did it ever occur to you I might just be looking for the right woman?''

''You have my permission to keep looking, cowboy.''

''Funny,'' Dave mused, ''I wouldn't have pegged you as a coward.''

Stiffening, she lifted her chin. Before she could lash out at him, he offered his own take on the situation.

''I don't think you're afraid of feeling hurt or jealous. You're afraid of failing. You like to win, Kate. You want to be the absolute best you can be at everything. Golf. Work. Marriage.''

''And that's bad?''

''No. That's good. Very good. You go into everything heart first.''

She was still stiff, still a little torqued at being

called a coward. Smiling, Dave brushed a knuckle down her cheek.

"The problem is, there are no guarantees when it comes to this love business. Not for Ryan and Jaci. Not for us."

"Who's talking about love?"

"I am. I think."

At her look of astonishment, his smile took a lop-sided tilt.

"I know. Half the time I'm convinced it's only plain old-fashioned lust. All I have to do is picture you in turquoise spandex and my throat goes bone dry. Then I watch you at work, see the sweat and long hours you put into this project, and lust gets all mixed up with admiration and respect and something I've had a hard time putting a name to."

"Dave, this is crazy. You can't... You don't..."

She stopped, drew in a slow breath, and adopted the gentle tone of a nurse addressing a seriously ill patient.

"Respect and admiration I appreciate. Lust I understand. I've felt more than a few twinges of all three myself where you're concerned. But love... Well..."

She glanced to the side, as if expecting the right words to materialize on the cool, crisp air.

"It's okay." A grin stole into his voice. "The idea kind of gives me goose bumps, too."

It gave Kate more than goose bumps. It shook her

right down to her boot tops. She'd worked so hard
at convincing herself she was just another trophy in
his collection, that one torrid weekend defined the
parameters of their relationship. It stunned her to hear
his feelings went deeper. And that they had confused
him as much as Kate's had confused her.

But love…

Her face must have expressed her welter of uncer-
tainty, doubt and wariness. Chuckling, Dave stroked
her cheek again with the back of a knuckle.

"I don't figure we'll sort this out tonight. Or next
week. Let's just take it a step at a time. See where it
goes."

"Where can it go?" Kate asked, echoing her conversation with Cari. "Once Pegasus proves his stuff,
we all head back to our separate units. Unfortunately,
I've discovered I'm not real good at long-distance
relationships."

"So you stumbled once. You didn't win. Does that
mean you won't ever get back in the race again?"

He knew what buttons to push, she thought rue-
fully. She hadn't liked being called a coward. Nor
was it in her to run away and hide from a challenge.
Particularly when the stakes were as high as these.

Could she love this man? Did she want to?

The answer was staring her right in the face.

"Okay," she conceded with something less than
graciousness. "Consider me back in the race."

"Good." With a satisfied smile, he slid a palm

around her nape. ''Just to make it official, here's the starting gun.''

''Hey!''

That one startled yelp was all she managed to get out before his mouth came down on hers. He kissed her hard and long, apparently determined to make up the ground he'd lost over the past few days.

His taste and his tongue sent little sparks of pleasure through Kate, heating her skin as they traveled her length. Dave added to the sensations by tunneling one hand into her upswept hair, wrapping the other around her waist and bringing her hard against him.

She curled her fingers into the soft, worn leather covering his shoulders. Her head went back, her chin tilted to find just the right angle. Within moments, she was breathless. Moments more, and she had to drag in big gulps of air when Dave broke off the kiss. She was still gulping when he reached down, hooked an elbow under her knees and deposited her on the tailgate with a small thump.

His skin was stretched tight across his cheeks, and his wicked grin signaled his intent even before he reached for the zipper tab at the neck of her flight suit.

''Dave!'' She grabbed his hands, stilling them. ''This is your idea of taking it slow?''

''I didn't say slow. I said one step at a time. And this, my very Kissable Kate, is the next step.''

He tugged free of her hold, got the zipper halfway

down, and bent to nuzzle her breasts. The warm, damp wash of his breath came through her cotton T-shirt. Shivers rippled over every square centimeter of Kate's body. Sighing, she gave herself over to the pleasure.

Her sigh got stuck in her throat as he took little nips through the soft cotton. Pleasure gave way to hunger and Kate knew she was in trouble. But when he eased the fabric off one shoulder, common sense told her it was time to put the skids on. Unfortunately.

"Surely you're not thinking we'll get naked out here in the middle of nowhere, are you?"

"Oh, babe," he muttered against the curve of her shoulder, "I'm way past the point of being able to think."

"Dave! One of Jill's patrols could come cruising by at any moment."

"Nah." He nibbled his way back up to her throat. "I said a silent prayer to the mountain gods. Worked like a charm last time."

"Dave, we can't. It's too cold out here. And I want an official measurement. I'm not sure this truck bed is really over the perimeter line. We might have to—"

Suddenly, she went stiff. Her breath left on a gasp.

"Omigod! There it is!"

With his face buried in the silky skin of her neck and his senses already close to overload, it took Dave a second or two to realize she wasn't referring to a hidden sweet spot he'd triggered by accident.

"Look!" Kate exclaimed, thumping him on the back with a fist. "Over there! One o'clock high."

Swallowing a groan, Dave dragged his head up and threw a look over his shoulder at the faint green glow just visible between the peaks.

"Now it shows," he growled, not at all happy to have his reasons for driving Kate out into the desert vindicated. She, on the other hand, could hardly contain her excitement. Wiggling free of his hands, she yanked at her zipper.

"We've got to get back to the site. I need to access the solar observatory database, see if they're taking readings on this."

Regret knifed into Dave at the disappearance of her lush curves. Despite her desire to return to the base, though, she couldn't seem to tear herself away. She stood transfixed, her gaze locked on the distant haze. Dave guessed she was trying to calibrate the intensity of the light waves dancing in the atmosphere and causing those weird, moving shadows.

He had to admit they were pretty riveting. He'd pulled some temporary duty at Elmendorf AFB in Alaska, had been treated to the spectacle of the northern lights. These weren't anywhere near as intense, but they gave Dave some insight into why the rumor had persisted for so many years that aliens had landed near Roswell, New Mexico. Folks had probably spotted a green glow much like this one and let their fears prey on them. They wouldn't have had the benefit of scientific data regarding sunspots and magnetic energy and solar flares. Kate and Stu Petrie had treated Dave to an extended discourse on the phenomena, yet the dancing lights still sent prickles of unease down his spine.

"Do you think that eerie glow will impact tomorrow's flight?"

The casual question masked a dozen different concerns. That the team maintain the tight test schedule. That they wrap up the air portion and move on to the sea trials. That Pegasus get a chance to strut his stuff before being harnessed for plow duty in the trenches. If things turned sour down in Caribe, the Pentagon might have to move troops in and noncombatant civilians out pretty quick.

Kate gave the haze a final, frowning glance. "At this point, I can't say what the impact will be. All I can do is check the data and see if the observatory is projecting any significant activity in the earth's ionosphere. We don't want to take any chances with you or with Pegasus."

She started for the passenger door, stopped, and spun around. Grabbing his jacket collar, she yanked him down for a hard, fast kiss.

"Particularly with you, flyboy."

Ten

Kate didn't sleep at all that night.

She spent hours hunched over her computer collecting reports from every possible source. The solar observatory in Sunspot had recorded an increase in ionization in the earth's upper atmosphere, but no disruption of satellite or radio communications as yet.

By morning, she was hungry, hollow-eyed and more nervous than she'd ever been before jumping aboard one of NOAA's planes to fly into the eye of a howling storm. She knew every piece of equipment aboard the specially modified P–3, knew just how it would respond when buffeted by hurricane-force winds.

In contrast, Dave was going up in a new vehicle with only one operational test flight to its credit. The contractor representatives were confident they'd shaken the bugs out of Pegasus during the research and development phase—particularly after analyzing the data from the loss of the first two prototypes and incorporating design changes. But there was a good reason why the military didn't accept ships or aircraft or other highly sophisticated weapons systems without extensive field tests. Real-world conditions too often caused failure of systems that operated flawlessly in a controlled R and D environment. And high-energy solar explosions were about as real world as it gets.

As a result, Kate approached the 8:00 a.m. pretest meeting with considerably less confidence than she had previous such meetings. She was one of the first to arrive at the small conference room in the Test Operations building. Depositing her laptop and stack of briefing books on the table, she nodded to Russ McIver.

"'Morning, Mac."

"Hi, Kate."

"Are you going to load Pegasus with the equivalent weight of a full squad this morning?"

"That's the plan. Any reason to change it?"

Kate bit her lip. Pegasus was designed to carry a maximum of twenty fully-equipped troops or their equivalent weight in cargo. This would be the first test of how the vehicle performed fully loaded.

"No," she said slowly, thinking of all the weight and drag Dave would have to compensate for, "no reason to change it at this point."

The marine went back to flipping through the PowerPoint charts he'd prepared for the prebrief. Too restless to sit, Kate poured coffee into a mug emblazoned with the Pegasus test-cadre shield. Dave arrived a few minutes later and joined her at the pot.

"You look dead," he commented, eyeing her drawn face. "Gorgeous, but dead."

"Thanks."

By contrast, she thought wryly, he looked good enough to eat. His blond hair still gleamed from his morning shower, and his blue eyes showed none of the red tracks Kate's did.

"Did you get any sleep last night?" he asked her.

"Not much."

One corner of his mouth kicked up. "Me, neither. That bit of unfinished business we started out on the perimeter kept me tossing and turning all night. We *are* going to finish it, Hargrave."

Kate didn't argue. Sometime during the long hours of the night she'd accepted Dave's challenge. She was back in the race. Despite the tension that knotted the muscles at the base of her skull, she flashed him a ten-gigabyte smile.

"If you say so, Scott."

The rest of the cadre filed in, dumped their briefing books and hit the coffee. Everyone was in place when Captain Westfall arrived at precisely 0800. Chairs scraped back. Officers popped to attention. Even the civilians stood as a mark of respect for the naval officer whose drive and determination fed their own.

"Good morning, ladies and gentlemen. Take your seats, please."

After another shuffle, an expectant silence settled over the room. Westfall's glance moved around the U-shaped table and settled on Kate.

"Before we get into the actual mission prebrief, I've asked Commander Hargrave to give you an update on recent solar activity. We'll make the go/no-go decision for today's flight after we hear what she has to tell us. Commander."

Kate took the floor. The data she'd pored over last night was pretty well burned into her brain. She could talk her subject from memory, but had prepared a computerized slide presentation for the test team's benefit. Her palm slick from a combination of worry and nerves, she pressed the remote. The first slide cut right to the heart of the matter. It showed a soft X-ray image of the sun's "busy" side, with swirls of black clearly visible against the brilliant red corona.

"The National Solar Observatory at Sunspot, just a little over a hundred miles from here, has been monitoring a buildup of energy in the sun's magnetic fields. This increase in energy could lead to a solar flare, such as the one shown on this slide. This particular flare is in what we call the precursor stage, where the release of magnetic energy has been triggered.''

Kate hit the remote again and brought up another slide. In this one, the dark swirls all but obscured the red ball.

''In the second or impulsive stage, protons and electrons accelerate to high energy and are emitted as radio waves, hard X rays and gamma rays.''

The next slide depicted a glowing red ball with only a few black swirls.

''In the final stage, we can measure the gradual buildup and decay of soft X rays. Each of these stages can last as little as a few seconds or as long as an hour.''

She had their attention, Kate saw. Dave had received much of this information during their visit to the observatory. It was new stuff for the others.

''Solar flares are the most intense explosions in the solar system,'' she continued, bringing up the next slide. ''The energy released may reach as high as ten-to-the-thirty-second-power ergs. That's ten million times greater than the energy released in a volcano, and we all know the devastation that resulted when Mount St. Helens erupted.

''The problem is when the intense radiation from a solar flare enters the earth's atmosphere. It can disrupt satellite transmissions, increase the drag on an orbiting vehicle and generally wreak havoc with anything electronic.''

"Oh, great!''

The muttered exclamation came from Jill Bradshaw, but Kate saw the same concern reflected in every face at the table. A click of the remote brought up a bar graph charting the sun's magnetic-field activity for the past two decades.

"Solar flares generally occur in cycles,'' she informed her audience. "As you can see, 2000 and 2001 were peak years. This was predicted and planned for.''

"Planned for how?'' Russ McIver wanted to know.

"A 1998 flare knocked out the Galaxy 4 satellite and disrupted some eighty percent of commercial cell phone and pager use in the United States. As a result, military and civilian communications agencies took a hard look at systems dependent on satellite signals and built in more redundancy. For example, radio, television, bank transactions, newspapers, credit card systems and the like are now spread across a wider spectrum of low- to mid-altitude satellites. Some might get knocked out, but the others would be at different points in their orbit and be protected from the solar blast by the curvature of the earth.''

Caroline Dunn sat forward in her chair. Her brown eyes grave, she studied the bar graph. "Looks like flare activity has been minimal since 2001. Are you saying there's a chance that could change in a hurry?''

"I'm saying there's a possibility," Kate replied carefully. She had to walk a fine line between predicting something that might not happen and minimizing the potential, only to have it blow up in her face. "Some of you may have noticed a green glow in the sky, similar to the northern lights only much less intense. It's caused by higher than normal ionization levels in the upper atmosphere.''

"High enough to disrupt communications or interfere with the instrumentation on Pegasus?''

Kate answered Dave's question as truthfully as she could. "Not at present.''

"But you're concerned another burst of ergs will come zinging my way?''

"Yes.''

They were speaking one-to-one now. The others were still there, within their field of vision, but relegated to the background.

"Pegasus comes equipped with a lot of that redundancy you mentioned," Dave reminded her. "Backup communications, laser-guided navigational systems, fly-by-wire manual controls in the event of hydraulic failure.''

"I know.''

"There's also the fact I'm a test pilot. I've logged over a thousand hours in both fixed-wing and rotary-wing aircraft." His lips tipped into a grin. "I also survived almost every natural and unnatural disaster you threw at me during those hours in the simulator.''

''It's the 'almost' part that worries me.''

''That part worries us all,'' Captain Westfall interjected dryly. ''I need your best professional guesstimate, Commander Hargrave. On the basis of the data available to you at this point, do you recommend we press on with the mission or scrub it?''

Kate fingered the remote. She knew the situation in Caribe had added to pressure on the captain. On them all. She also knew how little room there was for a slip in the schedule even without the Pentagon's latest worries.

She had to accept the possibility that one of the swirling sunspots could generate enough energy to fry every circuit aboard Pegasus. There was also the chance Dave and his craft could wing across a clear blue sky.

She didn't look at Dave. This was her time in the box. Captain Westfall would ask for his input in a few minutes.

''Based on all data currently available, sir, I recommend we continue the mission. I'll monitor the situation continuously. If I receive any indication of increased solar activity, we can terminate immediately.''

The naval officer accepted her judgment with a nod and turned to Dave.

''Captain Scott, you're in command on this mission. You've heard the risk assessment. You're also fully aware that you're taking up a craft that's still in the test stage. The call is yours.''

''I understand, sir. Taking educated, calculated risks is an inherent part of the test business. I agree with Commander Hargrave. As far as I'm concerned, the mission is a go.''

A small silence gripped the room. Although Westfall had deferred to Dave, none of the officers present thought for a moment the captain couldn't—or wouldn't—pull rank and overrule the pilot if he so desired. Kate held her breath, half hoping he'd exercise that authority.

But when he stood and moved back to the podium, Westfall gave the green light. ''Look sharp, people. We've got a mission to fly.''

They finished the prebrief just before eleven. Pegasus was scheduled to fly at noon. Dave skipped lunch to conduct a final walk-around of his craft.

Kate found him in the hangar. He and the crew chief assigned to the craft were inspecting the tail section yet again. The engineers hadn't been able to determine the source of the vibration Dave had experienced on the first flight and Kate knew it worried him.

She stood beside a rack of equipment, waiting for them to finish. Her recommendation to proceed with the mission hung like a rock around her neck. It was the right recommendation given the available data, but if anything happened to Dave…

Her stomach lurched. A tight ball of fear lodged in the middle of her chest. The stark, unremitting fear forced her to admit what she'd tried so hard to deny these past weeks.

She'd fallen for the guy. Big-time. Despite her doubts. Despite Denise and Alma. Despite the need to focus strictly on the mission. Sometime between the moment she'd spotted the long rooster tail of dust churned up by his pickup the very first morning he arrived on-site and their soiree out under the stars last night, she'd tumbled smack into love.

And now Kate was about to send him up into a sky that could go supercharged with as little as eight minutes' warning.

Swallowing the acid taste of fear, Kate waited until he and the crew chief had finished with the tail section and had worked their way up to the nose. They had their heads buried in a tech manual when she stepped forward.

"Got a minute?"

His smile was quick and for her alone. "Sure."

She couldn't say what she wanted to in front of the mechanic or the rest of the hangar crew.

"I need to talk to you." Snagging the sleeve of his flight suit, she tugged him across the gleaming, white-painted floor. "In here."

"Here" was the men's room, the closest private

spot in the huge hangar. Lifting an eyebrow, Dave followed Kate inside. Luckily, no one was at the circular urinal.

The latrine was as spotless as the rest of the hangar, but if Kate had had time, she would have chosen a better spot than a rest room smelling strongly of Lysol to let him know how she felt. The fact that time was fast ticking away made the place and the scent irrelevant.

"What's up?" Dave asked.

The smile was still in his eyes, but Kate sensed the edge behind the question. No doubt he thought she'd come to tell him the sun was still acting up and the mission had been scrubbed.

If only!

"I've been thinking about last night," she said slowly.

"That's funny. So have I." Reaching out, he snagged her waist and pulled her closer. "Finishing what we started out there under the stars tops my to-do list for after this mission. Unless…"

He skimmed a glance over his shoulder.

"We're in luck," he said with a hopeful waggle of his eyebrows. "The door locks."

"Cool your jets, cowboy. I didn't drag you in here to make mad, passionate love to you."

"Well, damn! And here I thought I was going to lift off with a smile on my face. Okay, I'll bite. Why did you drag me in here?"

"I wanted to tell you... That is..."

Even now it was hard for her to say the words. She was still confused by the feelings this man generated in her, still unsure of where they'd go from here. But she couldn't let him take off without letting him know she'd had a change of heart. She wasn't just back in the race. She wanted very much to win this one.

"Come on, Kate," he prompted, as curious now as he was amused by her temporary loss for words. It didn't happen often. "Spit it out."

"All right, here goes. I think... No, I'm pretty sure I love you."

Surprise flickered in his blue eyes for a moment, followed in short order by laughter and delight.

"Well, well! That makes two of us who are pretty sure. What do you propose we do now?"

"This, for starters."

Wrapping her fists around the collar of his flight suit, she yanked him down for a kiss.

It took him all of a second to get into the act. Wrapping an arm around her waist, he dragged her up against him. They were hard at it, lost in each other's taste and touch, when Kate registered the thud of a palm hitting the rest-room door.

"Oh! 'Scuse me, folks."

"Use the latrine across the hangar," Dave growled without lifting his head. "This one's busy."

"Right."

There was a hurried retreat, the sound of the door swishing shut. Kate closed her mind to the small sounds, the astringent tang of Lysol, to everything but Dave.

Finally, she had to let him go. He still needed to run through his preflight checklists and she had to pull herself together enough to face the rest of the crew. She couldn't believe how difficult it was to ease out of his arms.

"I'd better get back to Test Operations. I want to have a front-row seat when you take off."

"Aren't you going up in the chase plane?"

"Not this time. I want to make sure I have a land link to the solar observatory."

In case the satellite links took a hit.

She didn't finish the thought. She didn't have to. With a crooked grin, he reached up and tucked a stray tendril behind her ear.

"Don't worry, Commander Hargrave. You'll be right there with me, in my head."

And in his heart, Dave thought with a funny little jolt.

So this is what it felt like. As if he'd stepped into a zero-gravity chamber a half second before the floor dropped out from under him. For the first time in his admittedly varied experience, he found himself floundering, not quite sure how to propel himself forward.

He'd figure that out after his flight, he decided. When he had Kate alone, in the dark, in some place that didn't stink of industrial-strength disinfectant.

Eleven

Kate left Dave at the hangar and returned to the dun-colored modular building housing Test Operations. Inside was the small room lined with digitized display boards that functioned as the site's command-and-control center during tests.

Using her laptop, Test Ops' high-speed computers and a battery of communications devices, she set up a series of redundant links to various weather sources. A voice link to Stu Petrie confirmed her real-time access to data being fed back through the solar observatory's array of equipment.

"We've reoriented the Dunn Telescope," the scientist informed her. "We're recording every burp and bubble of energy emitted by the magnetic fields. So far, the propulsive activity has remained relatively stable.''

So far.

The caveat didn't reassure Kate. As Stu himself had pointed out to Dave, intense bursts of energy from the sun didn't take long to reach the earth.

''I appreciate you allowing me to tap into your data system, Stu.''

''There wasn't much 'allowing' involved,'' the scientist responded with a chuckle. ''The order came straight down from the top.''

Kate could hear the curiosity behind the comment. The observatory had been read in on the need for real-time information, but not the reason behind it. Neither Dr. Petrie nor his boss had been briefed on the specifics of the Pegasus project.

''I want to keep that data line open for the next few hours,'' Kate told him. ''I've also got landlines and radio communications available as backup.''

''Don't worry. We'll get the data to you if I have to bicycle it down the mountain myself.''

Kate bit back the reply that bicycling would get the information here too late for it to do any good.

''Thanks, Stu. Let's hope it doesn't come to that.''

Her glance went to the digital time display on the wall of Test Operations. Eleven-twenty. Dave would be airborne in less than an hour and back on the ground by 4:00 p.m. if nothing went wrong.

Her mouth set, Kate grabbed her mug and filled it to the brim with black coffee. The coffee wouldn't help the acid already churning away inside her stomach, but she needed something to take her mind off the clock.

Cari joined her and grimaced at the residue left in the bottom of the carafe. "I'd better brew a fresh pot. This looks to be a long afternoon."

"No kidding."

"He knows what he's doing, Kate."

That was the best the brunette could offer. She didn't try to minimize the risks. She couldn't. If Pegasus proved his capabilities in the air, Cari would be the next one in the hot seat. Responsibility for the sea trials rested squarely on her slender shoulders.

With the brisk efficiency that characterized her, she filled the pot, poured the water into the well and added a prepack of coffee. When the water had started to gurgle, she turned to Kate.

"Remember what Dave said. He's a test pilot. He's been trained to think fast and respond instantly."

Kate nodded.

"We'll bring him home." Cari gave her arm a gentle squeeze. "We have to. I'll be darned if I'm going to miss my ride."

By three-fifteen Kate was almost beginning to believe they'd make it. Her eyes ached from staring at the computer screens nonstop, her neck had a knot in it that wouldn't go away, and her stomach was pumping acid by the gallon. With one ear she listened to every beep and blip of the computers. With another, she monitored Dave's voice as it came over the loudspeakers.

"Chase One, this is Pegasus One."

"Go ahead, Pegasus."

"I'm climbing to thirty thousand feet."

"Roger, Pegasus. We're right with you."

Kate's glance flew to the computerized tracking board. The last test objective yet to be met was to ascertain the vehicle's performance with a full load at, or close to, its maximum ceiling. To accomplish that, Dave was now taking his craft in a wide, ascending circle high above the same resort the two of them had golfed in.

And made love in.

They'd have to go back to the Inn of the Mountain Gods, Kate thought, once this mission was over and she could breathe again. Dragging her gaze from the tracking board, she scanned the screen in front of her.

Suddenly, she froze. Her heart stopped dead, kicked in again with a painful jolt. Her horrified gaze ripped across the numbers painting across the screen once, twice. Then she was shouting for Captain Westfall.

"Sir! I'm declaring a weather emergency. We've got to get those planes down!"

His steely-gray gaze shot toward her. She didn't have time to explain.

"Now, sir!"

He nodded once and keyed his mike. "Pegasus One, Chase One, this is Test Control. Terminate your mission and return to base immediately. Immediately. Do you copy?"

"This is Chase One. We copy."

Kate's pulse thundered in her ears until Dave responded.

"This is Pegasus One. I copy, too, Control. How long have we got?"

Westfall looked to her. Hitting the switch on her mike, Kate delivered the dire news.

"Seven to eight minutes. If you're lucky. Get that baby on the ground!"

"Roger that."

After an instant of frozen silence, the entire test cadre shifted instantly into emergency mode. The engineers sent their fingers flying over keyboards to back up every bit of flight data. Captain Westfall ordered the crash recovery team to stand by. Doc Richardson alerted his medical personnel. Jill Bradshaw instructed Rattlesnake Ops to yank every off-duty military cop from his or her bunk and prepare them to secure a possible crash site.

Kate heard their voices, felt their tension jump through the air like some evil demon, but she focused every atom of her being on the computer screen in front of her.

The numbers were off the charts now. The energy burst was coming and it was coming fast. All indications were it would hit right above them.

She forced herself to think, to clamp down on the terror icing her veins and *think!* The whole upper ionosphere was about to go supercharged. Dave couldn't get above it. He couldn't get around it. His one chance, his only chance, was to find a protective shield.

The mountains! He could use the mountains! If the burst occurred over the desert, as was now looking more and more certain, the mountains *might* act as a shield. The high peaks had certainly contained the green haze Kate and Dave had observed last night.

Every nerve center in her body screaming, Kate raced to Captain Westfall. Somehow she managed to spill out a succinct, coherent version of her theory. The captain took all of thirty seconds to weigh the pros and cons. His jaw tight, he keyed his mike.

"Pegasus One, Chase One, this is Test Control. You have two minutes to possible system shutdown. We recommend you change course and drop down behind the Sierra Blancas. Use the mountains as a shield."

"Test Control, this is Chase One. We copy and are banking hard left."

"Roger, Chase One."

One of the dots on the tracking screen turned sharply. The other remained on a straight course. Westfall keyed his mike again.

"Pegasus One, do you copy?"

"Roger, Test Control. I'm initiating…"

The transmission ended in a screech of static. Kate's heart jumped straight to her throat as the lights in the control center flickered. Computers beeped. Displays went fuzzy.

A second later, the entire facility went dark.

Twelve

Deep, impenetrable blackness surrounded Kate. There was no light, not so much as a glimmer of a shadow, to give depth or definition to the windowless operations center. She heard a thump. A curse. A terse order for everyone to remain still until the emergency generators powered up.

Her heart measured each second with hard, excruciating thumps. After what seemed like a lifetime, a muted hum signaled that the backup generators were kicking in. Seconds later the lights blinked on.

The scene inside Test Control could have been crafted for a wax museum. Lifelike figures were frozen in different poses, their faces registering shock, dismay, determination.

Kate wrenched her gaze to the computerized tracking board. It was blank. Completely blank. Both aircraft had disappeared from the screen.

''Oh, God!''

Her agonized whisper seemed to break the spell. Suddenly everyone moved at once. Captain Westfall's deep, gravelly command brought instant order to the chaos.

''All right, people, listen up! Control, get on the radio and see if you can raise Pegasus and/or Chase One. The rest of you check your data terminals. I want to know if any of the computers aboard either aircraft are still transmitting.''

Officers and civilians scrambled to power up their computers. Kate had no sooner toggled the key on her laptop than the loudspeaker in the control center crackled. She spun around, her heart in her throat, as the loudspeakers emitted a loud burst of static. A few seconds later, a voice broke through the noise.

''...declaring an in-flight emergency. Do you copy, Test Control?''

Kate's nails gouged into her clenched fists. The voice wasn't Dave's. The transmission was coming from Chase One. Her momentary panic quickly gave way to a sharp, stabbing relief. If the C–130 was still in the air, there was a good chance Pegasus was, too.

The pilot's transmission was still echoing through the control center when Captain Westfall spun around and barked at the communications tech.

"Can you raise them?"

"No, sir. Not yet."

His jaw tight, Westfall could only listen with the others as the C–130 pilot tried to reach them again.

"Test Control, this is Chase One. We're transmitting on guard 121.5, using our backup battery."

Kate bit down hard on her lower lip. She'd spent enough time in the air to know 121.5 was a guarded frequency monitored around the clock by the FAA. It was always open, available for use by everyone from crop dusters to stealth aircraft in emergencies. The fact that the chase plane was transmitting via an open frequency told her instantly his secure communications had failed.

In the next moment, Kate and the rest of the team knew that the 130's comm wasn't all that had failed.

"Be advised we're declaring an in-flight emergency," Chase One repeated. "Our airspeed and altitude gauges are spinning like roulette wheels, the secure communications are fried, and we're flying by the seat of our pants. We're transmitting using our backup battery."

As Kate was all too aware, the backup battery contained only about thirty minutes of juice. The C–130 would have to go silent soon to conserve power for his landing.

"We had the target on our left wing…"

The transmission fuzzed, cut off for a moment, came back over the loudspeaker.

"...so we overshot the vehicle. Last reported sighting was at tango 6.2. I repeat, Control, tango 6.2."

Pegasus! He was referring to Pegasus. Kate's gaze whipped to the wall map that divided the vast site into specific patrol areas. Tango 6.2 was to the southeast, where the mountains trailed off into desert.

"This is Chase One, terminating transmission."

Kate chewed on her lip again until she tasted blood. A hundred unanswered questions thundered through her head. Had Dave made it to the mountains? Had the peaks shielded him, as they apparently had the C–130? Or had the chase aircraft overshot its target vehicle before Pegasus reached the granite peaks?

That question, at least, was answered a long, agonizing twenty minutes later.

The burst of solar energy fried communications towers and knocked out commercial radio, TV and cell phones in most of southern New Mexico. Buried cables were protected, although the switchers that routed calls took severe hits. Some calls went through. Others ended in static.

Hardened military communications fared considerably better. Jill used her radio to direct her people to activate the site's disaster-response plan. Within moments, each of the senior test-cadre members was supplied with a hand radio and could communicate with their counterparts in other agencies.

After several frustrating tries, Kate managed to get through to the National Solar Observatory. She was taking a fix on the exact area affected by the burst when Jill came rushing back into the control center. Her face set in tight lines, the military cop relayed the news they'd all been dreading.

"A local sheriff just notified the FAA of a possible downed aircraft. The air force picked up on the notification and relayed it to us. The craft was spotted going in just before the sky turned green."

Kate's chest squeezed. She couldn't move, couldn't breathe.

"The sheriff reports a column of black smoke rising from the approximate location," Jill continued grimly.

Captain Westfall clenched his fists. "Where?"

"Sector tango 6.2, sir."

Since the energy burst had fried the instruments in the chopper assigned to the Pegasus site, the initial disaster-response team was forced to employ land vehicles. Kate's duties didn't call for her to be part of the team, but no one, Captain Westfall included, challenged her determination to join the convoy. She raced out of Test Operations to retrieve her sidearm and survival gear.

Two paces outside, she skidded to a stunned halt. Jill was hard on her heels and almost ran over her.

"Some show, isn't it?"

Swallowing, Kate took in the green and yellow waves undulating across the sky. Normally the scientist in Kate would thrill at such a unique display. At the moment, she could only curse herself for underestimating their potential severity.

Sick over her miscall, she gathered her gear and ran to Rattlesnake Ops, where the convoy had already formed. Two Humvees, a wide-track fire-suppression unit, and specially modified all-terrain vehicles with machine guns mounted on the hood.

"I'll take the lead ATV," Jill informed the hastily-assembled response team. Her blond hair was swept up under a Kevlar helmet. She wore a bullet-proof vest under her battle-dress uniform. Her sidearm was holstered on her belt, and she'd slung an assault rifle over one shoulder.

"Our navigational and comm systems depend on satellite signals," she said tersely, "so we'll have to do this the old-fashioned way, using maps and compasses. Rattlesnake Four, you and your squad take the first Humvee. Doc, your medical response team have the second. Commander Hargrave, you're with the medical team. Mount up."

Jill had worked a deal with the military cops up at Kirtland Air Force Base in Albuquerque to modify the Hummers' engines. They'd required the increased speed to keep up with Pegasus during his land runs. Even with their modified engines, though, the vehicles couldn't chew up the desert fast enough for Kate.

It took the small convoy almost thirty minutes to reach the foothills of the Sierra Blancas, another twenty to hump through them to reach Tango Sector.

Less than two hours had passed since they'd lost contact with Pegasus. Every minute of those hours was etched into Kate's soul. She felt as though she'd aged a hundred years by the time the driver of her vehicle shouted to the passengers in the back.

"We're seeing a plume of black smoke dead ahead. It appears to be rising from a narrow gully."

Cody Richardson shouted back the question that burned in Kate's throat. "Any sign of the vehicle or the pilot?"

"Negative, sir. Major Bradshaw has just signaled to us to kick into overdrive. Hang on to the side straps, folks, it's going to get bumpy."

Ten bone-rattling moments later, the Humvee jolted to a halt. Kate was almost snarling with impatience as she waited for the rear tailgate to let down and the others to pile out. Disregarding the hand Cody held out for her, she jumped out and hit the ground with a jar.

Even before she raced around to the front of the Hummer she could smell the burning engine fuel. No one who'd ever survived a crash—or assisted at a crash site—could mistake that oily, searing stink. Her first glimpse of the dense black tower of smoke billowing into the sky sent her heart and her last faint hope plunging.

"Oh, God!"

The billowing cloud blurred. Hot tears burned Kate's eyes. A scream rose in her throat, aching to rip loose.

Shuddering, she fought it back. She had work to do. They all did. She swiped an arm across her eyes, swallowed the sobs that tore at her throat and reached a shaking hand into the pack containing a small, portable respirator and an oxygen pack. Anyone going within a hundred yards of that raging cloud of smoke would need both bottled air and protective clothing.

The crash-recovery team was already dragging on their shiny silver protective gear. Suddenly, one of them jerked an arm toward the fire.

"Isn't that Captain Scott?"

Kate spun around, terrified he was pointing to a charred, blackened body. She couldn't believe her eyes when she saw Dave scrambling down the side of the gully.

"'Bout time you folks got here!"

Keeping well clear of the smoke, he broke into a long-legged lope. Kate wasn't as restrained. She dropped her gear bag and charged toward the gully full speed.

The idiot was grinning!

Grinning!

That was the only thought she had time for before she plowed into him. He rocked back, steadied, and wrapped his arms around her.

The sobs Kate had forced down just moments ago ripped free. She couldn't hold them back, any more than she could keep from gripping his flight suit with both fists, as if to make sure he didn't disappear into that black cloud.

"I thought you were dead!" she wailed against his chest.

"It was touch-and-go there for a few minutes," he admitted, his voice a deep rumble in her ear. "But I'm okay, babe. I'm okay."

She didn't know whether it was his steady assurances, the knuckle that rubbed gentle circles on her spine or the abrupt arrival of the rest of the team that made her realize she had to get herself under control. Gulping, she pushed the sobs back down her raw throat and swiped her forearm across her eyes again. Dave kept one arm around her as the others peppered him with questions.

"How did you get down?"

"Did you have to bail?"

"Have you sustained any injuries?"

The last came from Cody Richardson, and Kate's euphoria took a swift nosedive. He'd insisted he was okay, but in tough, macho pilot lingo, that could mean anything from scratch-free to protruding bones. She pulled away to take a closer look while Dave parried their questions with one of his own.

"Did the C–130 crew land safely?"

"As far as we know," Jill informed him. "They

declared an in-flight emergency and were flying by wire, but we've received no reports of a downed aircraft other than yours.''

Dave let his breath whistle out. ''Good. They were a couple of hundred feet above me when the sky lit up. I was afraid the mountains didn't give them the same protection they did me.''

''Some protection,'' Jill murmured, her glance going to the burning funeral pyre.

''That was a hell of a call on Captain Westfall's part,'' Dave commented, ''sending us down behind the hills like that.''

''Captain Westfall didn't make that call,'' Jill informed him. ''Kate did.''

''No kidding.'' He squeezed her waist. ''Thanks for saving my butt, Hargrave.''

''To paraphrase a certain pilot I know, your butt is eminently savable, Scott. I'm just sorry I couldn't save Pegasus, too.''

''You did.''

''Huh?''

That less-than-intelligent response won her a quick grin.

''I lost some instrumentation, but I managed to bring him down. He's parked about a hundred yards down the gully.''

Kate's gaze whipped to the noxious black column. ''But the fire... The smoke.''

''My communications were fried. I didn't have any

way to signal my location, so I emptied some fuel from the vehicle, piled up brush and started my own personal bonfire. I figured someone would spot the smoke.''

Kate couldn't quite take it in. Dave had survived. So had Pegasus. They'd both come within a breath of having their wings permanently clipped, but both had survived.

''Now what do you say we put out the fire,'' he suggested briskly, ''throw a security cordon around the craft until we can get it back to base, and make tracks. I didn't have any lunch. I'm hungry.''

Still in a daze, Kate shook her head. ''He's hungry,'' she echoed to Jill. ''He wants food.''

''So feed him,'' the cop replied with a grin. ''Doc, one of my troops will drive you, Kate and Dave back to the site. I'll stay with the craft until it's secured.''

Dave released her long enough to retrieve the gear bag he'd stashed well away from the fire before rejoining her at the Hummer. Kate ducked her head and prepared to scramble inside. He helped her with a firm hand under her elbow and a whispered promise that raised instant goose bumps.

''Food isn't all I'm hungry for, my very, very Kissable Kate.''

Thirteen

It was long past midnight before full communications and power were restored at the base, Dave had finished debriefing his extraordinary flight, and Pegasus was once again bedded down in his gleaming white stall.

Two days, Captain Westfall announced to his weary staff, before the maintenance crew could replace every circuit that had blown in the test vehicle.

"That puts us behind the eight ball again on the sea trials. We'll have to cut the water-test phase to the bone," he instructed Cari. "I want you and Major McIver in my quarters at oh-seven-hundred with a restructured schedule."

Cari gulped. "Yes, sir."

"You can work here," Westfall said. "We'll clear the conference room and let you have it. The rest of you…" His glance roamed the circle of military and civilian personnel. "Get some rest. You'll need it, because once we leave for the coast and begin water trials, the pace is going to pick up considerably."

Kate couldn't imagine how! In the past two months, their tight-knit group had warded off an attack by a mysterious virus, lost one of their members to a heart attack and survived a megaburst of solar energy. Oh, yes, they'd also proved Pegasus could run like the wind and fly with eagles.

She muttered as much to Jill as the group dispersed. With a shake of her head, the site's chief of security agreed the pace was plenty fast enough for her.

"At least I'll get a break when we move down to Corpus Christi. We'll be operating out of a navy base, so they'll have overall responsibility for security. All I'll have to do is keep unauthorized visitors away from our little corner of the base."

"Wish I could look forward to a break. We'll be arriving at Corpus smack in the middle of hurricane season. Cari might just get stuck swimming Pegasus through gale-force seas."

"If anyone can do it," said a deep voice behind them, "Cari can."

Both women turned to find Doc Richardson waiting patiently for Jill to finish her conversation. Kate looked past him at the still-dispersing group.

"If you're looking for Dave," the doc commented, "he said to tell you he had something he wanted to take care of and he'll see you later."

"Later?"

It was close to 2:00 a.m. Kate hadn't slept more than an hour or two last night. Worry over that damned solar flare had kept her tossing and turning. That, and Dave's challenge that she get back in the race.

"Did he say how much later?"

"No." The doc's cheeks creased in a grin. "But he did ask me to keep Jill occupied for an hour or two."

"And your reply was?" Jill wanted to know.

"I told him I'm here to serve. Come with me, Major, and I'll let you look through my microscope."

"The last time I did that, I ended up flat on my back. With a virus," she tacked on dryly, but she didn't protest when Cody steered her toward the dispensary.

With a surge of excitement that chased away her weariness, Kate headed for her quarters. She had a good idea why Dave had asked Cody to keep Jill busy for an hour or so. If she moved fast, she could get in a quick shower and change out of the flight suit she'd been in for going on twenty hours now before the man arrived at her quarters.

She should have known she couldn't outrun a sky jock. Dave was already there. In her bed. Wearing nothing but a grin and his watch.

"What took you so long?" he complained.

Laughing, she leaned against the doorjamb. "How the dickens did you beat me here? Cody said you had some business to take care of."

"I did."

With a jerk of his chin, he indicated the box of condoms he'd invested in at the Inn of the Mountain Gods. They'd run through a respectable number of them, but there had to be at least five or six left.

"After our little adventure today, I just wanted to make sure we had plenty of backup and redundant systems."

Kate groaned. "That's the worst attempt to get a girl in the sack I've heard yet."

"I can do better," he assured her. "Come here, KK, and let me whisper in your ear."

"KK?" she asked, then remembered the nickname he'd bestowed on her. "Never mind, I got it. Move over, DD. Give me room to sit down and take off my boots."

He obliged, edging his hips to the far side of the twin bed. Kate sat on the edge, brought her foot up and let her glance sweep the length of his lean, muscled body. Her bootlace snapped in her fingers.

Dave didn't help matters by propping his head in

one hand and playing with her hair while she shucked
her boots and socks.

"DD, huh? Let me guess. Darling Dave, right?"

"Wrong."

"Daredevil Dave?"

"Not even close."

"Gimme a hint."

"No hints. You have to figure it out for yourself."

Kate stood, unzipped her blue flight suit in one
fluid move and stepped out of it. Her sports bra and
panties followed her cotton T-shirt to the floor.

"In the meantime, cowboy, why don't we see just
how redundant your systems are."

Very redundant, Kate decided some hours later.

She lay flopped across Dave's chest, boneless with
pleasure and so sleepy she couldn't pry up even one
eyelid. A dozen solar flares could have burst above
her and blazed across the night sky and she wouldn't
have seen them.

She did, however, hear Dave's soft whisper as he
eased her off his chest and into the crook of his arm.

"This is one race we'll both win, Kate."

*   *   *   *   *

From *USA TODAY* bestselling author

MERLINE LOVELACE

TO PROTECT AND DEFEND

Trained to put their lives on the line.
Their hearts were another matter....

A Question of Intent
(Silhouette Intimate Moments #1255,
November 2003)

Full Throttle
(Silhouette Desire #1556, January 2004)

The Right Stuff
(Silhouette Intimate Moments #1279, March 2004)

Available at your favorite retail outlet.

Silhouette®

Where love comes alive™

Silhouette®

Desire.

presents

DYNASTIES : THE DANFORTHS

**A family of prominence...
tested by scandal, sustained by passion!**

Man Beneath the Uniform
by
MAUREEN CHILD

(Silhouette Desire #1561)

He was her protector. But navy SEAL
Zachary Sheriday wanted to be more
than just a bodyguard to sexy scientist
Kimberly Danforth. Was this one seduction
Zachary was duty-bound to deny...?

*Available February 2004
at your favorite retail outlet.*

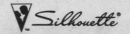

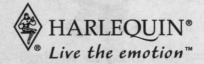

COMING NEXT MONTH

#1561 MAN BENEATH THE UNIFORM—Maureen Child
Dynasties: The Danforths
When Navy SEAL Zachary Sheriday was assigned to act as a
bodyguard to feisty Kimberly Danforth, he never considered he'd
be so drawn to his charge. Fiercely independent, and sexy, as well,
Kimberly soon had this buttoned-down military hunk completely
undone. But was this seduction one he was duty-bound to deny…?

#1562 THE MARRIAGE ULTIMATUM—Anne Marie Winston
Kristin Gordon had tried everything possible to get the attention of her
heart's desire: Dr. Derek Mahoney. But Derek's past haunted him, and
made him unwilling to act on the desire he felt for Kristin. Until one
steamy kiss set off a hunger that knew no bounds.

#1563 CHEROKEE STRANGER—Sheri WhiteFeather
He was everything a girl could want. James Dalton, rugged stable
manager, exuded sex…and danger. And for all her sweetness, local
waitress Emily Chapin had secrets of her own. One thing was
perilously clear: their burning need for each other!

#1564 BREATHLESS FOR THE BACHELOR—Cindy Gerard
Texas Cattleman's Club: The Stolen Baby
Sassy Carrie Whelan had always been a little in love with Ry Evans.
But as her big brother's best friend, Ry wasn't having it…until Carrie
decided to pursue another man. Suddenly the self-assured cowboy was
acting like a jealous lover and would do *anything* he could to make
Carrie his.

#1565 THE LONG HOT SUMMER—Rochelle Alers
The Blackstones of Virginia
Dormant desires flared the moment single dad Ryan Blackstone
laid eyes on Kelly Andrews. The sultry beauty was his son's teacher,
and Kelly's gentle manner was winning over both father and son. A
passionate affair with Kelly would be totally inappropriate…and
completely inescapable.

#1566 PLAYING BY THE BABY RULES—Michelle Celmer
Jake Carmichael considered himself a conscientious best friend. So
when Marisa Donato said she wanted a baby without the complications
of marriage, he volunteered to be the father. Their agreement was no
strings attached. But once pent-up passions ignited, those reasonable
rules were quickly thrown out the bedroom window!

SDCNM0104